The Labyrinth Beckons

CATASTROPHE INCOMING: VOLUME IV

AIMEE DONNELLAN

ISBN (paperback): 978-1-7385843-7-6

ISBN (e-book): 978-1-7385843-8-3

Editor: Quinton Li (https://www.quintonli.com/)

Cover artist: Katelyn McNeely (https://twitter.com/tacticiankate)

Cover typographer: Inorai (https://www.fiverr.com/inorai)

Continuity Expert: Ty Donnellan

www.aimeedonnellan.com

Contents

The 'Catastrophe Incoming' series

1. The Chase Begins

2. The Collection Awakens

3. The Survivor Stands

4. The Labyrinth Beckons

5. The Spirit Torments (October 26th 2024)

6. *Title to be finalised* (Feb 2025)

7. *Title to be finalised* (June 2025)

8. *Title to be finalised* (October 2025)

Books 9-12 will be released in 2026 and 2027, exact months to be confirmed.

Content Warnings

This work contains: depictions and descriptions of violence and blood, frequent coarse language, and non-explicit sexual references.

IMAGE DESCRIPTIONS

BOOK COVER

A depiction of a brunet person with brown skin and a brown right eye. The angle shows their right side, while they face a pink crystal in a wall with great concern. Their hands, nose and cheek show some grime and blood. Behind them is a green flame in a brazier and stone walls.

The text reads: The Labyrinth Beckons, Catastrophe Incoming: Volume IV, Aimee Donnellan

Map of Qelandia (and Kequm)

A map showing the Republic of Qelandia, with the city of Cypethus near the top on a shoreline and the northern path of the Grand Highway. To the west is the town of Hanos, with the Labyrinth marked in the nearby hills. On the other side of the map, Cythos sits furthest south with the town of Vincium slightly further northeast, near the edge of some mountains. Almost directly north, but on the Theocracy of Izirm side of the border, sits the city of Kequm. The Grand Highway comes northward, near Hanos, but not near Cythos or Vincium, and meets with the northern stretch near the top of the map. A mountain range—holding Grena's Collection—separates Kequm from this section of the Grand Highway.

CYPETHUS
THE GRAND HIGHWAY
KEQUM
REPUBLIC OF QELANDIA
GRENA'S COLLECTION
THEOCRACY OF IZIRM
THE LABYRINTH
HANOS
VINCIUM
CYTHOS

To anyone who ever wanted to kiss the evil lady and wondered if it would be so bad if they did, and was relieved that no consequences would be real for them. If only Lark had such a luxury.

The Story So Far

While the war against dragons rages across the Theocracy of Izirm, and the Republic of Qelandia, the bishops of the Theocracy are trying to find a way to an abrupt end. The adventurer Lark and their friend Wren, are enlisted by a deputy bishop of the Scholar god, Andrian, to help recapture a murderous mage, Nightingale. Lark, who has a complicated history with Nightingale, wrestles with complex feelings as they try to bring her in. They are also distracted by snippets of information on *The Ascension Project*, a secretive endeavour that holds the hope of the Theocracy's future and somehow requires a revered warrior of the Warbringer, Ser Palla, to succeed.

Ultimately, Nightingale's trickery and an impossible decision result in the murderer's escape from Kequm.

Upon using their Wayfinder (a magical teleporter in their possession) to follow her, Lark and Wren find themselves in a magical Collection in the Qelandian mountains. No Nightingale in sight, but malevolent magic ready to strike down everyone inside. They meet Reverie, a musical adventurer and mage (and her horrible companion Ferdinand, a magical goose).

After recruiting Reverie into their murderer catching team and realising that the malevolent magic might be connected to their current mission or the war, they use the Wayfinder to once again try and jump to Nightingale's location.

Instead, they end up in a village under siege from bandits... bandits who are known to Wren, having hit her town a year before. They are led by her uncles. With the help of Lark and Reverie, Wren is able to help the village survive the last attack and fights one of her uncles until he is forced to flee. They learn that her uncles have been hired to find a labyrinth near the town which is supposed to hold an extremely valuable magical object, but someone else has been through looking for the same information. Nightingale, with the ability to get information from corpses, killed the town librarian.

Now, Lark and Wren and Reverie seek the labyrinth... which is where our story continues.

Dramatis Personae

(In Order of Appearance)

Lark - *they/them* - adventurer and follower of the Scholar god, Gifted mage of the Scholar

Wren - *she/her* - a small town blacksmith's daughter, powerful swordswoman

Reverie - *she/her* - latest in a long line of adventurers, musician and Disciplined mage

Ferdinand - *he/him* - cursed goose tied to Rosetia family, formerly [REDACTED] [REDACTED] of [REDACTED]

Nightingale - *she/her* - serial murderer and collector of secrets, Gifted mage of [UNKNOWN]

Chapter 1

A LABYRINTH, BY NATURE, is not a straightforward thing. A labyrinth that contains one's murderous ex... well. Lark is not sure a word exists to encapsulate how opposite of straightforward that is. A labyrinth hidden in rural hills. A mysterious magical power source. Protection in the form of trials of character. On any other day, Lark would be skipping.

This week, however? Their world is upside down. Inside out. Their heart yanked out of them only to be assaulted and scrutinised by almost everyone around them.

Being foolish enough to still love Nightingale fiercely. Feeling as though they are constantly letting down Wren, and every wonderful thing she represents. Not succeeding in helping Andrian and the people of Kequm when it was so, so important to not fail. Palla had been so quick to judge how Lark would not take Nightingale's life, as though such a choice could ever be simple or easy.

In all of that turmoil, there are two points of peace. The way that despite it all, the care in Wren's eyes has not dimmed when she looks at them. And, the bizarre joy that comes with arguing with Reverie, their most recent friend. Reverie is so impressively aggravating that when she manages to pull Lark into another pointless argument, Lark has no space in their brain to linger on any of the awful things happening.

Lark would call it serene, if that were not blatantly absurd. How funny, too, that their closest friend is the epitome of calm and confident, and that their newest provides an opposite but equally helpful energy.

The latest argument is, naturally, who knows more about labyrinths. Only Reverie Rosetia could have the ego to try and go against a Seeker of the Scholar on this matter. But in a barely shifting landscape of hill and grass and cloudy blue sky, here they are with nothing better to do.

"Plays are hardly known for their historical accuracy, Rosetia," Lark says.

"Not all knowledge is fact, sometimes it's understanding," Reverie retorts.

"How can there be understanding without fact?"

"Very easily!"

"Give an example."

Reverie rolls her eyes at them. "Okay. Example. Only the greatest mages can make spells that manufacture or trigger from romantic love. Because that would involve, you know, quantifying it. But almost any adult you meet could tell you either what it feels like, or what it seems to be based on how they've watched other people. The *knowledge* of how love works is a mystery, we have to trace it by movement in our minds and bodies at the tiniest level. But we understand it. Even if we don't know how it works."

Of all the things to use as an example, Lark had not expected *that*. And of all the topics they could have landed on, this one is perhaps the one they are the least equipped to handle today, when Nightingale's face and laughter are echoing in their head whenever it gets too quiet.

Their chest is tight—not because of their binder, which has been delightfully exciting to wear again after days of running around—but in a visceral reaction to Reverie's words. Lark's mind tries to twist the argument in every possible way, to refute it, on base instinct, but it is not so easy.

In the end, their answer is not a rebuttal so much as a tired closing statement.

"We don't always understand it." Lark says, staring at Reverie and her blue aura of curiosity. "Sometimes we just feel it." *And wish we didn't.*

In a rare moment for Reverie, she does not answer. Her large golden eyes blink at them, newly thoughtful and always more understanding than Lark expects, and yet—there is nothing in her aura that suggests she either disagrees or agrees, a strange detail that leaves Lark with an uncommon guess about someone and their life.

Reverie has not known romantic love enough, deep within herself, to have her own true opinion on it.

"What do the plays say about that?" Lark asks.

She grins, a second late like she's surprised by it coming to her mouth. "Oh, so many things. But... I liked how you said it."

With marvellous timing, Wren whistles from the top of the next hill to get their attention.

"Is that the pair of hills you told us to look for?" Wren asks.

Lark dashes up the slope to stand next to her, ignoring the binder's warnings against such rapid bursts. They dig in their pocket for the map, which had been a secret of a nearby town's librarian who had been a victim of Nightingale's search.

The only good thing to come of Nightingale plucking secrets from the heads of corpses is that it makes her lazy when it comes to searching for physical information. Thus, leaving the paper map still hidden and ready to be found when Lark and the others had reached the librarian's office after her.

Wren is absolutely right, with a keen eye for images and context. Twin hills, with one marked with an oval on the map—in reality, it is a mere outline in the distance, but definitively *there*.

"Looks good," they say, and let their feet carry them downhill at a quickening pace.

By the time the trio close the distance to the marked hill, some minutes later, a large metallic construct at the base confirms it. The circular door blocks their entrance, intimidating and floral in the same instance, especially when at second and third glance, the flowers are... wrong. Too strange. The detail of the adornment and patterns are jarring, almost beautiful but actually unnerving. A closeness to reality that is not quite right.

"It's—" Reverie stops short, pausing to remove her horse Melora's bridle and kiss her nose. She goes to turn back to the door when Melora neighs in protest at the goose honking in circles around her. After a second of Reverie staring at him, the goose stops as if yanked by an invisible chain. As if nothing at all has occurred, Reverie looks back to the metal door. "Yeah, okay, still weird."

"It's just flowers," Wren says. "What's so strange about that?"

"The design's just..." Reverie makes vague gestures. "Not quite what you'd expect, if you're used to Elven art."

"Because it's *Old* Elven," Lark says with a nod. The current Elven Empires are heavily influenced by the fey, with their religion centering them, but outside influences are still tangible. Those outside influences cannot be seen in the door's design. The Old Empire was different; they ruled everything they touched, considered nothing else. "Most of these hidden places are. Remnants of the old empire that was stretching and stretching until... well. Until whatever made them all vanish."

"Yeah, that was bizarre," Reverie murmurs. "My family has always wondered about the timing. It wasn't long after we all got our mundane magic."

Everyone has a little. A few gimmicks, passed down through families, nothing near what a studied or manifested mage could do, but often something vaguely useful. Lark has always been able to spark a tiny fire if the right fuel is ready to host it, which is useful when one travels to remote places.

Lark knows they should be paying more attention to the Labyrinth. That is, however, impossible to do when Reverie is talking about the origin of common magic, one of Aboria's greatest historical debates, like it was a casual uncontested fact.

"Um," Lark says, slowly, "How could you possibly know that?"

"Well, apparently the appearance of the common magic is what kicked up the first fuss in the empire," Reverie says with a shrug. "The third Rosetia heir was around when the mundane magic came in—we have her journals. It seems like the empire launched a lot of new projects *really* fast right after, like they were trying to work out where it came from. I wonder what they found... if it's what made them disappear."

Lark, for several moments, has no words. They can only gesture between Reverie, the goose, the sky, and the world itself around them all.

"Every historian under the sun is busy wondering why they vanished, and there's a chance the answers have been in your family records *this whole time*?" Lark eventually squeaks.

Reverie crosses her arms over her chest. "Well, no. It didn't seem like the ones running the show were talking to their people, let alone their neighbours. The Rosetias used to be based in the Federation, you know. It was part of the Old Empire back then, but no one there was getting told anything. Just that... one day, they were all gone."

"But to even know that *that's* when the common magic came in, with certainty," Lark says, with astonishment. "No one else even has confirmation that it hasn't always been around, it's just been a strong theory based on ancient writings and their references to—"

Wren coughs into her hand, politely. Lark hadn't even noticed her moving to look over the door's design, so they are half alarmed.

"There's writing on this," she says, patient but pointed. It's a kind way of her telling them that they've gotten sidetracked.

And a brilliant way of pointing out something they've missed. "I'm guessing you'll be able to read it?"

"Oh! Marvelous," Lark says at once, hurrying to have a look. They'd been debating doing a full tactile analysis of the door itself, checking for any curious ridge or hidden levers, and that's still a tried and true method for old mysterious doors... but they'll try the route of written clues first. The historical discussion will have to wait. It cannot delay their encounter with Nightingale forever. "Yes, Old Elven dialect. I think I can make it out... something about being polite. A request. Bit unhelpfully vague, isn't it?"

"Please tell me we don't have to bargain with a door," Wren groans.

Reverie leans over Lark's shoulder to have a look, her hair brushing close to their nose and leaving them with the scent of honey and orange blossoms as she pulls back a moment later.

When she speaks, it is not in universal common, but in fluid, lilting Elvish. The words that mean *open, please.*

Several mechanisms of the door click and slide in rhythmic succession, and Lark barely jumps back fast enough to avoid getting hit in the nose as the door swings open.

"Huh," Reverie says, with a grin. "I didn't think that was going to work."

Chapter 2

If there is anything Lark has learned in dealing with strange magical things, it is that *anything* is worth a try. Especially when considering that enchantments are generally done by people, and thus enchantments often follow the logic of a person rather than an object or otherworldly creature.

"Manners will get you everywhere," Lark tells Reverie. "Well done." They look to Wren, whose incoming question is obvious in the dip of her eyebrows. "She asked it to open. Nicely."

"Wait. Does that mean Nightingale said the word *please*? Out loud?" Wren asks, incredulously.

"I'm sure it was with great reluctance," Lark says with a snort. "But even she can't kill a door. Though she might have tried."

It feels good to giggle with Wren over something so silly. Making her laugh feels special, and they cannot help the small sense of pride they feel for making a joke at Nightingale's expense.

As the trio step inside, the sunlight is quickly drowned in the depths of the cavernous space. It extends before them, into the dark, until lanterns spark with bright green flames on the walls either side of them. The ceiling is twelve feet high at the lowest point, curving upward in an elegant arch. The entrance hall's walls are twenty feet apart and covered with artwork, intricate designs that tell a story of the research and creation of a great power—something that, if the depictions are in any way accurate, amplifies the magical abilities of anyone that wields it.

"Oh, so *that's* what this thing does," Lark says. "What fascinating possibilities. No wonder powerful people with grand plans for the war are probably trying to get their hands on this." They simply will not think about exactly which people those might be, lest the possible answers be too awful to contemplate for long.

No matter how many times Lark stands in a place of the past, where centuries before others stood, they feel torn. Not quite here or there, itching to explore until they collapse, until they find some secret in the walls and writings that no one else has. Wanting to beg the ghosts of history to impart some wisdom, some insight into their lives.

They've always felt more at home among the echoes of the dead than among living people.

"How old is all this?" asks an awed Wren.

"At least six hundred years old," Lark says. "Incredible, isn't it? If we'd never been to that tower, we'd have never known this was here. There should have been *some* reference to it in the Scholar's archive, but I've been over every inch of their magical artifacts section, I'd definitely remember coming across records of anything like this, and if Nightingale and *I* couldn't find it, then—"

"What if *she* found it?" Wren asks. "And hid it from you?"

The pair of questions nearly stop Lark in their tracks. They want to argue that it couldn't be true. But Nightingale feigning ignorance around a magical artifact in a ruin is *exactly* how they ended up here. Cursed, torn apart, seeing things in the world no one else can. Even if that particular untruth had been before the murders had started, this would simply be another in a growing collection of lies.

They meet Wren's eyes, let out a soft sigh, and choose to let the defeat of it speak for itself.

There is no guidebook on what to do, when one unexpectedly receives remarkably specific and unprecedented abilities that feel as though they were chosen just for you. History from objects, secrets from corpses. All in the name of gathering information. And then their curses, just as tailored. Nightingale, forced to record every new thing she learns, forever. Lark, with no choice but to deliver information right to someone's face, or not at all.

The pair of them had gone straight back to the university of the Scholar. But the moment they began making verbal inquiries with some of their most trusted ex-Professors, self-imposed silence became the safest option, as each question was met with confusion and scrutiny that neither of them cared for. Better to turn to the safety of the unspeaking, written word.

Once Nightingale had shown her new, true colours, and Lark dragged her to prison, the archive had called to Lark again. They went over it book by book, page by page, trying to find an answer to fill the screaming void in their chest.

For all Lark knows, Nightingale had found an exact reference to this labyrinth, and removed it without their knowledge so that she could one day claim its power. It is within the realm of possibility, easily. Lark knows that simply saying *but that doesn't sound right* will do nothing. Gut instinct can only go so far, but tends to loathe being ignored.

Wren reaches for Lark's hand and gives it a squeeze. While Reverie moves on to examine some of the murals further in, they hang back.

"Sorry," Wren says. "You know I have to ask."

"Of course you do." Lark grips her hand tighter. "I actually… rely on it. Or I'm going to, today."

"Are you okay?"

Lark shakes their head and hates how a chill runs through their whole body. "I'm terrified. Before, there was no warning, and then there was no time. But knowing I'll have to face her at any moment now…"

"Look on the bright side," Wren says. "She won't be expecting the goose."

A snort escapes Lark and they smile after, gratitude warming the icicle in their chest. "That's true. The goose or the new mage." Lark looks to Reverie for a moment, observing how her fingers trace across the lines of the paint and carvings without quite making contact, reverence in every step. Then, back to Wren, who briefly followed their gaze. "What do you think of our new additions?"

"I think she keeps your brain busy," Wren says, with a shrug. "And we're lucky to have another mage who wants to help. She means well, right?"

"I think so," Lark says. "On all accounts. I suppose I'd just gotten used to it only being the two of us."

"Me too." Wren smiles, only to glance down at their still joined hands and release Lark's abruptly. Her cheeks are pink and Lark pretends not to notice as she turns away. "Anyway. Labyrinth."

As they come to join Reverie, she smiles at them both.

"So, what do I need to know about Nightingale, anyway?" she asks. "Other than, you know. That we need to stop her. You said you need to know who helped her escape. I'm good at getting information out of people, if you think that'll work."

"Maybe," Wren says, narrowing her eyes. "She likes the sound of her own voice."

Reverie cocks an eyebrow. "Not a bad trait by default."

"No, but there's... you," Wren says, with a gesture up and down Reverie's general person. "And then there's whatever horrible shit she's saying at any moment."

"Yeah?" Reverie glances at Lark, who nods. "Good. I can work with that."

"She's not going to be interested in you," Lark tells her, and continues before she can open her mouth to argue. "She's regarded anyone who isn't me like an insect for years now. Don't take it personally. If that's possible, for you."

Reverie snickers. "Oh, she can *try* to ignore me—"

"If your plan is to annoy her into paying attention to you, know that she might simply stab or suffocate you as a means of silence."

Reverie blinks at that. A pale yellow of fearful worry pulses around her, only to be repressed a moment later. Almost all of her negative emotions immediately are—only two never fade from her aura completely. Lark had told her, when they had first met, that one emotion remained visible at all times. A half truth. The other had not been relevant at the time.

The guilt could have implicated her in the Collection, if she had not been obviously working to assist everyone else there from the start. It's dark grey, tinged with faint red that implies it comes from a place of anger, suits her ill, but another colour stops it from clashing directly with the pink and gold of her. A black as deep as a starless night, one that clings to her even more closely than the guilt. Every emotion's colour varies from person to person, especially when it can be tied to other feelings, but something about the magic of the dragon eye means that Lark never has any difficulty deciphering it.

The deep black around Reverie is spite. A spite so powerful that Lark can only be perplexed.

Lark, these days, is no stranger to auras not matching a person's manner or face. But for it to shroud someone who is so bright and musical and brilliant? It raises many questions. None of them appropriate. That's one of the downsides to this power. The knowledge without understanding, the always wondering and never asking.

"Just be careful, Reverie," Lark says to her, putting a hand on her shoulder. "As you said. You're too pretty to die here."

Reverie's fear gives way to one of her astonishing smiles. "I'm too pretty to die in a tiny village with a dirt road. Dying in a place of ancient magic and mystery would make a good song."

"Counterargument, not dying at all," Wren suggests.

"Because I'm pretty?" Reverie asks, fluttering her eyelashes in her direction.

Wren shrugs. "Because you're a good person who helps people. But sure, because you're pretty."

Lark's gaze travels around the space, and finds shadows that descend—a staircase. Upon walking closer, the braziers on the walls light with that same eerie green flame. The air in here tastes old, and Lark cannot help how it throws them back to some of their most fascinating journeys and kicks up further excitement in their chest. Next to the stair entrance is a plaque bearing more Old Elvish writing.

Caution to those who journey below
The amplifier will go only to those
who prove the strength of hearts and minds
Alone, success is inconceivable
Together, the trials must be shared

The braziers are curious, so Lark reaches for the nearest one and concentrates. The history is so old it is almost tinged by time itself, and Lark absorbs many colourful elven visages of ancient warriors entering the labyrinth, and at least half walking out with defeat slumping their shoulders. (Which raises questions about the other half, that's for sure.) Then come a few non-elven figures, youth putting a bounce in their step. They do not come back out.

At the very end is something much more familiar. The brazier activates as a woman with curls of dark red hair descends the stairs.

There you are.

Chapter 3

When Lark lets go of the brazier, they find Wren and Reverie standing right beside them, close enough to make them startle at the unexpected proximity.

"Ah!"

"Sorry," Wren says, as Lark tries to get their flailing limbs under control and settles themself by grabbing their collar and ruffling it. "You were taking longer than usual."

"Yes, well, this brazier is about five hundred years older than most things I touch, at least," Lark says. They cough into their hand, only to despair upon realising how dusty it now is and wiping it on their coat. "Anyway. Nightingale's definitely already inside."

"Did chatting to the brazier tell you that?" Reverie asks with a giggle. "This creepy staircase is so cool."

"Objects don't chat, they just show me things," Lark says.

Reverie nods. "… is that how you knew that thing in the Collection was the eye of a god? Wren wouldn't tell me how it worked, but if objects can tell you things—"

"They show me their history."

An odd laugh rocks Reverie, while Wren walks down the stairs ahead of them both.

"All that talk outside about my family having access to forgotten history," Reverie says, with disbelief. "And you can do *that*?! How?"

Lark almost tells her something which would half explain it. But in the face of such a terrifying day, where everything will be out of control, this secret sits too powerful on their tongue. And they deserve some fun before the day turns horrendous.

They lean into Reverie's space, making her still, and whisper in her ear.

"Won't it be so much more fun if I let you figure it out, Miss Rosetia?"

Reverie pulls back to meet their gaze, eyes dark and intrigued. "Oh, fuck you," she says, but she's grinning.

Lark bites their tongue before they can be tempted to find a clever response to that. Instead, they turn and focus on following Wren down the stairs. Their foot meets white feathers instead of stone step, and they immediately lose balance, falling against the wall.

"Why is there a goose here?!" Lark cries, while Ferdinand honks with delight.

"I ask myself that every damn day," Reverie says, kicking Ferdinand down the stairs before following his trajectory. The goose is too busy laughing to do anything but bounce and cackle, which might be the most unnerving part of any of it, actually.

Lark curses the biological reaction of a racing heart in the face of a near-falling session. There are plenty of *reasonable* things to be concerned about today that do not involve tripping on steps due to geese. It is also not lost on Lark that the last time they descended a staircase into darkness, dreading seeing Nightingale at the bottom, things had turned out much worse than expected. Their skin prickles with rotten anticipation.

As they reach the final step, they are in a simpler stone corridor where they can fit comfortably three abreast and even Wren might struggle to touch the ceiling if she gave it a running jump. Roomier, all things considered, than Lark's expectations.

The braziers frame a wall someway ahead with a gem embedded in its surface. The gem is an astounding shade of blue. It glimmers in the flickering light, and above it, Old Elvish script reads 'The Trial of Knowledge'.

"I was expecting a door," Reverie says, as she reaches the level ground a step behind Lark. "This is obviously the way to go—look at the framing. But also... it's a wall."

She's right, of course, and yet on the corridor wall to their right there is a large, arch-like indent in the wall, several inches deep. Lark frowns at it.

"What about that indent?" they ask Reverie. "Looks almost like a door to me. But your point stands. Why frame it this way?"

Reverie's eyes follow Lark's gaze, but flick back to them in an instant. "Uh... what?"

"You don't think so? I know it's a strange placement, but—"

"No, I just can't see what you're talking about," Reverie says. Her puzzlement is genuine, flaring all around her. "That's a stone wall. There's no indent."

Wren frowns and looks between Lark and the wall. She walks up to the latter. "Is it here?"

"Yes!" Lark says, with relief, until they see the hesitance creasing her brow and circling her head in soft wisps. "Oh. You can't see it either."

Wren shakes her head, her smile gentle. "No. But I believe that you can."

"It's right there. Big arch, wide enough to fit two people, several inches—"

Wren places her hand on the space and it stops in what looks to Lark like thin air, but where the wall would be if the entire thing were as uniform as Reverie claims. Lark sucks in a breath. Several moments pass, and nothing changes.

"Thanks for checking," Lark says with a lick of their lips. "I suppose this is just... one of those things. Like the puppeteer, back in the Collection. I wonder what it's for."

"Do you hallucinate... often?" Reverie asks. The tact injected into her tone is cloying, but Lark makes a strong effort to appreciate the intention behind it. She doesn't know what she's talking about, after all.

"What's more worrying, the idea that I'm seeing things which aren't there, or that you're not seeing things that are?" Lark asks with a cocked eyebrow.

Reverie blinks, wordless, and Lark takes a petty comfort in it.

"I'd say the gem is our best bet forward," they continue. "It's got the big sign, after all. We'll worry about walls and doors and which is which *after* we've done the trial."

"So you think it might be a door?" Wren asks.

"Gods, I hope so, or this is going to be a deeply underwhelming labyrinth," Lark says to her, snorting. "In all seriousness, it must be, or else Nightingale would be here. Now, trial of knowledge, is everyone alright if I give this one a go?"

As expected, no protest comes, and Lark strides forward to do the only thing that reasonably makes sense: they put their hand on the gem.

Magic meeting magic is always fascinating. It's like chemistry, and this magic is old enough that for a moment as it reacts to the magic within Lark, they are thrown back to when their entire existence had turned upside. It had also involved touching something old and powerful in a ruin of the Old Empire. It had been a rush of everything everywhere and all too much, and had knocked them out cold in an instant.

The familiarity makes Lark want to flinch for fear of another upheaval they could not weather, but there is no such reckoning. Instead, there is greeting. Not quite words, but a feeling of acknowledgement slipping over their mind. Then, a question of what comes next, the same as if it were to ask if they are here for the trial.

Lark thinks of the affirmative as strongly as possible, and this time words *do* come. First in an Old Elvish that Lark struggles to follow, before the magic twists the words into innate translation. It's not Aborian Common, or Izirm Dialect

Common, but something that transcends exact words and focuses on meaning.

This is the trial of knowledge. In order to pass, answer questions three. One: if you mix root of elm and flower of firescale, what do they become? Two: what form of fabric best holds illusion enchantments, and why? Three: in the southern land of Znikadia, how is their singular god otherwise known?

Lark's heart hammers in their chest at the pressure, but they take deep breaths and remain as calm as possible. The first is simple. Nightingale had picked the firescale flowers while Lark dug up the elm root from a nearby tree, all to ensure that Lark's questionable plan of putting a dragon eye in their own eye socket didn't result in a nasty infection.

"Root of elm and flower of firescale make a sterilising poultice," Lark says. They can speak freely for once, as there are no eyes for them to require meeting.

"Huh?" Wren asks.

Lark waves a hand behind them to try and convey she need not worry, even though their speaking answers to unspoken questions might be unsettling.

The second question is delightfully difficult. Enchanting is a specific discipline, not quite magecraft and yet not detached from it, and requiring a whole theory of its own. Lark is no enchanter and never will be, but their unconventional background is their saving grace today. One of their old guardians and teachers, a woman by the name of Professor Elisha Myron, had been an expert seamstress—not just that, but a seamstress who worked with mages. Lark had never failed to listen when she was speaking, her words always captivating no matter the subject.

"The fabric that best holds illusion enchantments is lace, as the magic can be intertwined with the thread while it is being woven."

Lark waits a beat, and when nothing signifies failure, they release a breath and prepare to answer the last question. They had been confident in the answer, but not the explanation also required.

The third question is actually the easiest, as it is a matter of global politics that has been more unchanging in the last six centuries than anything else.

"The god of Zhikadia is otherwise known as their Emperor," Lark says.

The existence of a supposedly reincarnating living god is a hard thing to forget, once you learn about it. Lark would give almost anything for a chance to learn more, but has yet to think of a way that a Seeker of the Theocracy poking around a foreign religion centered around a political leader *wouldn't* cause a diplomatic incident.

After giving the final answer, there is a moment where nothing happens at all. It is an awful, terrible moment where Lark comes back to the explanation about the lace and considers every possible way they could have gotten it wrong, or worded it better, and how would Elisha or Lillian have explained it. For all their knowledge, they can never be precise with words when it matters—

The gem glows. It is so bright that Lark has to tear their eyes away, and the wall shimmers before it vanishes altogether. The gem remains exactly in place, but now suspended in the thin air.

No more words come from the gem, but Lark gets a sense of congratulations before they remove their hand from it.

"Thanks," they say, and cannot resist patting it like they would a friend's shoulder.

"I have questions about lace," Reverie says from behind them.

Lark turns around, a grin pulling at their lips. "Truly, a sentence more people should say. Let's walk and talk."

Unfortunately, there is only so much to be said about lace's magical capacity when neither participant of the conversation knows anything tangible about enchanting. Still, engaging with another curious mind, however briefly, is always good for the soul.

Once the lace conversation dies, the silence that follows invites glances from Wren. Glances from Wren invite crescendos to Lark's heart, and not for any fun reasons.

"Are you ready?" Wren asks. "I know you don't like thinking about Nightingale, but she's down here, and if you're not ready—"

"I'll be ready," Lark says, and wishes with everything they have that it is the truth.

"I'm ready—" Reverie tries to chirp, only to be interrupted.

"You're not," Wren says, blunt but not unkind. "She'll kill you if she thinks it'll be funny. Be very, very careful what you say. She can teleport with her magic, she's faster than you can believe."

"Right," Reverie says, swallowing.

"It's how she stayed out of our reach back in Kequm."

Lark puts a hand on Wren's shoulder. "But she also played us."

"She did," Wren agrees. Her expression is grim. "So we need to do better this time."

The words hit heavy, like sinking stones. Lark recalls standing with her in a street of Hanos, to her saying how what happened in Kequm had not been good enough even if it had been their best. It was not unlike being struck in the face, but also a needed wakeup call.

"We'll do everything we can," Lark promises. "We'll try to make it good enough, this time."

Wren nods, her hand coming up to squeeze Lark's where it still rests on her shoulder. Her half-smile is tired. "We're taking her in this time."

"How, exactly?" Reverie asks, with wide, dramatic hands. "Are we tying her up? Or are we supposed to, like, take her *out*?"

Lark winces. "We're not supposed to do anything, actually. The Theocracy is supposed to be sending mercenaries to catch her, because they don't think I'm able to be objective enough."

"Well, fuck that, because we're already here," Reverie says, her eyes flashing with fire. "And fuck objectivity. No one ever won anything by being objective. You get places by giving a shit. By caring so much you feel like you've been impaled. If she's your ex? It has to be you."

Bewilderment washes over Lark at her words. It is then soothed by camaraderie and comfort, coming in waves one after the other. Despite their arguments, it's a validation to hear something which supports their gut, the part of them which knows it has to be them, even when logic no longer supports it. Lark always tries to follow logic, but when it comes to Nightingale that is no longer possible. They feel what they feel. Their gut urges them on in a way they cannot justify or quantify.

And somehow, in an instant, Reverie agrees. Perhaps it is not actually a good thing. Perhaps it will doom them. But in this moment, it feels so *warm* to be understood.

"Thank you," is all they can say. It comes out soft, a little choked.

"Sure," Reverie says. "What can I do to help?"

"Don't give her any reasons to kill you faster," Lark says with complete seriousness. To their surprise, Reverie does not quip in response. She only nods.

"We can do this," Wren says, and Lark is unsure of who she is addressing, anymore. "We have to."

"Worst comes to worst, I'll throw one if my boom balls in her general direction," Lark says, to lighten the mood. "Or, you know, at her face."

It's an obvious lie, but it has the desired effect of Wren choke laughing and Reverie letting out a near shriek.

"One of your *what*?" Reverie says, cackling.

"Lark has explosives in their pockets, like a reasonable person," Wren explains.

Reverie beams at Lark. "You're so *bizarre*. What the fuck?"

There is little to do but shrug and laugh a little more.

The three of them continue on, and the silence that envelops them might be the most comfortable they have shared since becoming an odd little trio. Lark basks in it. It may be the last semblance of peace before a trial mishap or Nightingale shattering it all.

The map which had led them here had given no indication of what happens if a trial is failed. Lark is often more optimistically inclined, but not enough so to believe that there will not be repercussions in this instance.

The trio turn corner after corner, lighting braziers all the way. It occurs to Lark that this does not make for a subtle approach, since they have no way to stop the pre-enchanted lighting of the braziers, apparently triggered by mortal proximity.

For once, however, fortune smiles upon them. Long before they reach the next trial, there is a distinct sound of cursing in a lilting, smooth cadence more coloured with fury than Lark has heard in years.

Lark's hand darts out to grab Wren by the armour plate to stop her from walking further. She half turns, a sound of protest in her throat, before she stops and cocks her head at the sounds.

"... is that *her*?" Reverie whispers from next to Lark.

The voice is unmistakable. Lark once relished hearing it curse people stuck in their ways, usually professors without care for her out-of-the-box research projects. Later, the voice cursed Lark instead.

"It's her," they murmur, nodding at Reverie. "The braziers will give us away, but if we're lucky, she might be facing the trial, preoccupied enough that she doesn't notice. Let's go slow, and quiet, and get as close as we can."

There is a moment of nodding among themselves.

Then, the deafening honk of a goose echoes through the passage, louder than anything has ever had a right to be.

Chapter 4

Silence follows. Or rather, silence punctuated by awful echoes of the obscene honk, and then shattered by goose laughter which vanishes a moment later. Lark's eyes are closed as they bite their tongue and curse the day they agreed to take on Reverie without working out ground rules for the goose.

The cursing ahead of them has stopped. This immediately validates Lark's caution; like a canary in a mine, no singing from Nightingale is a sign of danger. They peek through their eyelids and sure enough see Reverie with her hand in the air, completing a motion that must magically dismiss her strange companion to some sort of *elsewhere*. Something to ask about later.

"Why did we bring him down here at all, again?" Lark whispers to her.

"Because if I keep him in his pocket dimension hell all the time, he's *worse*, and micromanaging him is so fucking tedious.

I have to let him out at least to start," Reverie says. The words make enough sense, but she looks as though she desperately wishes she'd changed up her process today. "I'm so sorry."

The apology might just be the most genuine thing that has ever left her mouth in Lark's presence.

"It's quite alright," Lark says, even though it may not be. "I can't say I've any idea how I would handle being in your position."

"He *can* be useful," Reverie mutters.

Lark glances at Wren, who has crept to the next turn in the passage to peek around it, and gives a tentative thumbs up without moving from her station. Briefly reassured, Lark looks back to Reverie and can only sigh.

"Rosetia, respectfully, I'm not your boss, your keeper, or your mother," they say to her. "If we survive this Labyrinth and Nightingale I can assure you I won't be holding any of this against you." She looks dubious, so they cheerfully add, "And if we don't survive, then I shan't be able to chastise you for it."

Reverie's lips twitch despite themselves, and Lark reaches out to pat her shoulder. They have a thousand burning questions remaining about Ferdinand, and they know now is not the time. The itch to know everything about *everything* can be genuinely exhausting.

The three of them return to their creeping, sans goose. Lark makes sure to go first. If Nightingale is on alert for people coming up behind her, Lark is the only one who will survive her preparation.

A step around a corner. A flash of dark red. A prick of sharp metal at Lark's neck, brought up fast and stopped only just in time. There is a fleeting vindication in seeing surprise in Nightingale's lilac eyes.

"Darling," she says, leaping backward just as Wren steps up next to Lark. "I didn't know it was *you* making that racket." Her eyes flick behind Lark, no doubt to Reverie. "Careful. Your pet collection is growing. That one's a bit much, don't you think?"

Nightingale is never one to stay on the backfoot for long. It's a layered deception, a complex dance. Her words spell ignorance, while her eyes say something else. She is searching the catalogue of her memory, perhaps triggered by the pink and gold demonblood in proximity to a honk of a goose.

Meanwhile, as she walks backward, towards the trial too far off for Lark to be able to read its label, her body is coiled like a spring. Ready to escape or seize the upper hand in whatever way suits her, at a moment's notice.

On their right is another circle in the wall, shimmering and enigmatic just like the one before. Nightingale's eyes flick to it, then back to Lark. As they had suspected, what is invisible to Wren and Reverie can be seen by Nightingale. Why is it hidden to most? What *is* it about these odd, unconnected things that are seen only by a few?

"Does she honk?" Nightingale asks Lark. One of her weaker deflections, as if Lark cannot see her hand scribbling in the notebook on her thigh. The comment actually cements Lark's certainty that she is writing about a Rosetia in Lark's midst.

"Quite often, actually," Lark replies. They put their hands behind their back and take a step forward to test the waters. Nightingale mirrors the movement, taking another step backward. "How goes the trial?"

Nightingale's eyes narrow. Her hair is a mess of curls, like it gets when she's been running her hands through it endlessly as she searches for an answer which eludes her. (Or, once upon a time, when Lark was free to put their hands through it instead.) Its state alone gives Lark the answer they seek.

Gloating is an uncouth thing. Unattractive in the extreme. But after the crushing defeat Nightingale served Lark when they last crossed paths, it is impossible not to rub it in. Just a little.

"Why don't you give it a try?" Nightingale asks. "We can compare notes."

Lark barks out a laugh. "And have it decide we're all on the same team, getting you closer to a power source you can't be trusted with? Hardly. This is as far as you get. You really will be coming with us, this time."

"Bold words for someone with deeply stabbable friends," Nightingale snorts. "All I have to decide is... which first? Flowers, or pastel vomit?" Her eyebrow quirks. "What are you doing with a Rosetia, anyway?"

"You know my family," Reverie says. It's not a question.

"I know more about everything than you could imagine," Nightingale says with a roll of her eyes. "But your grandmother—I'm guessing she was your grandmother—stumbled into my path in a ruin. One of the only people I couldn't dispatch. A shame. She clearly had some great secrets in that noggin of hers."

Reverie makes a noise of derision. Nightingale's eyebrow lifts even higher, until it almost disappears into her hair.

"You're not quite as impressive, unfortunately," she says to Reverie. "Or... perhaps *fortunately*, in my case—"

Her magic flashes and she leaps forward into a dark portal which swallows her form even as Lark shouts in futile protest. She appears next to Reverie, quill at the ready—and the pommel of a sword slams into her temple.

"Predictable," Wren tells her.

Nightingale sways on her feet. Her quill hand has dropped to her side, and she steps backwards into another portal when Wren makes a grab for her. She appears further down the corridor, clutching her head.

"Huh, you *are* tough," Wren says, eyebrows up.

Nightingale mock curtsies, a bit lopsided, her glower the icing on top.

"Trouble with the test, dear?" Lark asks. "What was it? How to be a nice person?"

Another thing that ought to be beneath them. A jibe, a petty thing. But after all the grief she has caused them, they cannot help it. The last thing they expect is how her face twists with rare, genuine disdain directed absolutely at them. It says more than any words could.

"Oh my goodness, I was *joking*," Lark says with delight, a high giggle escaping their throat. It likely sounds ridiculous, but in this moment they simply do not care. "Was it really?"

"Selflessness," she says through gritted teeth. "I knew what it wanted to hear, but I suppose it knew it wasn't what I would actually do. Rotten, clever magic."

Wren cackles. "So it knew you were a lying piece of shit. Nice."

"That's a funny way of saying you want a quill in your neck, flowers," Nightingale growls, with a flex of her fingers. She glances at Lark. "Does this one have a death wish?"

"No, I imagine she's just tired of your nonsense, as I am," Lark replies. "I've had a perpetual headache since we last saw each other, you know. I don't intend to keep it, so I'll do whatever I can to dispatch it, even if that means extreme measures."

A perpetual headache is actually a mild way of putting it. Lark suffers from full bodily protest, their head and chest and gut screaming at the entire scenario since they left Kequm and knew the business remained unfinished. Mortal consciousness can be such a pleasant, reasonable thing.

Nightingale scoffs, her arms crossing over her chest. "And what is your idea of extreme measures, darling? Hitting me with a prayer book? Telling me off using real curse words?"

Lark takes their time answering. Or rather, they take several deliberate steps away from their friends and towards Nightingale, in order to hide the fact that a good answer eludes them. They know she must be captured, but not how, but they can't *say* that—

They are saved from providing an answer. Not, however, by a miracle of any kind but a metal monstrosity surging into the corridor. It comes right out of the wall, bursting into the space with no warning—

Wait. Not out of the wall. Out of the shimmering part that only Lark and Nightingale could see. A head almost as tall as Lark's entire body, eyes flashing with something which is not life but a crafted mimicry, mouth wide with razor sharp metallic fangs.

A snake. But not the kind of serpent any of them could claim to have seen before. Lark presses themself against the wall to avoid being crushed by it, as half of the corridor is filled by its inordinate size. Such a thing could only be crafted with specific function, and in a place such as this, said function could only be a small number of possibilities.

The construct turns to Nightingale and snarls; it is a horrid sound, artificial and grating and echoing off the stone in a way that very nearly *hurts*.

Sometimes things become very clear very quickly. Function: predator. Nightingale: prey. Lark: running. They don't exactly mean to. Their feet push off the wall and floor before their brain can think anything through, their body sliding under the creature's great head and towards Nightingale.

Towards the woman they simply cannot, will not allow to perish. Later, they'll probably justify it with *if she is dead, we'll never know who freed her, who wanted this power source*. But it simply isn't that in this moment.

It's as simple as: *No. No, not her.*

Clarity, the ill-timed bastard that it often is, comes a moment after they skid to a stop next to Nightingale, specifically in the moment where they stare up into the giant mouth and Wren screams their name somewhere behind.

"Ah," Lark says. "Hello—" The snake charges and Lark pushes Nightingale out of the way, barely rolling in time to avoid the thing's teeth in their side. "You're rather marvellous and terrifying!"

They leap back, Nightingale thankfully moving with them, and summon a shield to buy them a moment to breathe, a golden barrier of energy focused around the two of them.

"You know, there was a funny gong noise when I failed the trial," Nightingale says, as the snake tries to eat them through the shield. Lark tries not to shudder at the intimate look they get at its terrifying array of teeth through the translucent golden magic.

"Oh, *now* you tell me," Lark says. They wince as the snake bashes its head against the shield, and know it will only hold against a few more strikes. "Well, it's specifically going for *you*. So what? Punishment? Eradication of the unworthy?"

"Do you *hear* yourself sometimes?!" Nightingale snaps.

Another ram from the construct. The shield falters for a moment after and Lark focuses every spare bit of concentration they have into having it hold just a bit longer.

"I'm speaking on hypothetical behalf of a missing, ancient civilisation who don't give a singular fuck what happens to you, none of this was *my* idea," Lark says, so outraged they can see their own aura in the corners of their vision. "Would you like me to let it *tear you apart*?

It's at that moment that the shield vanishes, probably because Lark is no longer focused at all, and the serpent tries to eat Nightingale before she can answer. On what can only be impulse, Nightingale shoves her quill up into the roof of its mouth, and two regrettably predictable things happen.

One: Nightingale's quill snaps in an instant because it's a tiny piece of metal. Two: Nightingale gets a metal fang in her upper arm. All around poor show.

There are many fascinating ways to say the word 'fuck', but the way Nightingale utters it with such self-directed exasperation is one of the most magical things Lark has witnessed.

The snake tries again, of course, and Nightingale clutches her bleeding arm and stumbles into a portal just in time to avoid its strike, coming out a few feet down the corridor.

"Lark!" Wren has drawn her sword, and is barely visible behind the serpent's huge body. "What's the plan?"

Inspiration strikes at the same time the serpent's tail does, the latter walloping Lark in the stomach with battering force while the former comes as the horrendous realisation that the best plan may be the most reckless one.

For it to work, however—

Lark sends up a quick prayer and then dives at Nightingale. It is a tackle that only works due to the element of surprise, and they immediately wrap their entire arm around her face, covering her eyes as much as they are able. In the same moment Lark frantically looks past the monster, seeking a glimpse of Wren or Reverie's faces so as to free their tongue.

Flowers. Freckles. Green eyes.

"Get ahead of us!" Lark shouts. "Take the trial, get to the centre first—"

The serpent strikes, but misjudges the angle and falls just short of Nightingale's shoulder, still blinded by the shadow. Nightingale, however, gets her broken quill perfectly into Lark's arm and stabs them through the sleeves of their shirt and jacket.

Never have the words 'fuck off' so desperately wanted to leave Lark's mouth. They lose sight of Wren and have to roll themself and Nightingale to dodge the snake's next bite attempt. It's an awful thing to ask of their friends, Lark knows, but it's the only way to keep them out of Nightingale's reach and to keep Nightingale barred from the prize.

"Wren, come on," Reverie's voice says, and Lark can just make out the sound of hurrying footsteps.

They could cry with relief, but instead have to keep holding Nightingale, which is an increasingly dangerous and painful process between the snake's teeth and her quill. Lark can heal a bloodied arm, but their beautiful coat may never recover.

They dodge the next attack—almost. Its teeth close on Lark's ankle and they yell at the top of their lungs. It nearly matches the verbal curses Nightingale is hurling at an impressive rate.

Time gets a bit blurry, and there are many things Lark would *like* to say but cannot. Finally they hear a shout from Wren.

"We're through! Don't die or I'll kill you!"

Very motivating, Wren, thanks. Lark tries to get a view of the wall to see when it will close behind them; they had not thought to look behind them after going through the first gate. But by all logic it must, if Nightingale had come first. If it isn't a quick thing, this will turn to disaster near instantaneously.

One second. Roll. Struggle against Nightingale's pointy elbows. Four seconds. Five. Six. Desperation, tinged red and drowning them both. A bite that scrapes down Nightingale's back and makes her shudder in Lark's hold. Lark craning their neck to see, and at ten seconds exactly, the vanished wall flickers back into sight with the crystal dimmed.

Lark releases Nightingale and throws themself as far away from her as possible. Nightingale recovers just fast enough to dodge the next bite, but now she's on her own again with the serpent focused on her and her alone, Lark's proximity no longer interfering.

Nightingale's hair is a mess of mussed waves falling across her face and shoulders. Through the strands, her glare shines bright.

"I'm sorry, but really everything you've ever done is the only reason *that* was necessary," Lark says to her.

She times her next teleport well, waiting until the serpent is *almost* on her before appearing next to Lark, close enough to make them jump a mile. "Why is everything always my fault?"

Lark turns their head to meet her gaze again, stepping back as they do so, to stay away from surely incoming metal teeth. "Because you do terrible things that you know are terrible, decide not to care, and act surprised when reasonable people *do* care!"

"I'm *sure* you used to be more interesting than this, you know. You sound like my father. Life is sacred, we must never extinguish it, blah blah blah—"

In a perfect moment of karma, Nightingale mistimes her next teleport and the serpent manages to close its mouth around her leg. She yells and manages to find time to meet Lark's eyes again.

"Happy now?" she demands.

"Yes, I'm delighted to have been separated from my friends and left alone with the person who has hurt me most in the world," Lark says.

Their words are all they have to protect them. They're not lies, but imply a simplicity of position which is impossible for Lark to occupy. Alone with Nightingale, any kind of protection is a necessity. Most people need protection for their major arteries or airways, while Lark needs protection for their traitorous heart.

Nightingale manages to get her leg free. She teleports on top of the serpent and tries to use her broken quill to carve into its head.

"How do you kill a *metal snake*?!" Nightingale screeches, perhaps to herself, or perhaps to Lark. One has to admire how she persists in using the quill stub to pry at the silver scales.

Lark has no answer to that question. But it is becoming increasingly clear that one of them is going to have to find out.

Interlude

I - WREN

IT IS HARD TO say which is more absurd: Lark's plan, or the fact that Wren actually goes along with it.

It is a war of many things. Of Reverie's hand tugging on hers, of the clanking and grinding of metal on the stone floor and the pained shouts of Lark as gods only know what is happening to them, and every part of Wren demanding she run into the fray and pull Lark out of it. But if Wren does not listen, then that pain is for nothing.

If Lark's plan is to stop Nightingale getting what she wants, Wren has to respect that, and that plan must come before all else.

Wren runs for the crystal despite all her base instincts. She looks to Reverie as a way of asking which one of them is going to attempt the trial, and the other woman's eyes flick to the text above the gem. *The trial of selflessness.* Reverie's teeth bite into her lower lip and she shakes her head.

It's not encouraging, but it's an answer. There is no time to argue.

Wren slams her hand onto the gem with splayed fingers. Immediately, her nerves coil through her arms and shoulders as an unfamiliar sensation touches her mind.

Lark had made this look so simple.

Wren expected words, or a voice. She gets neither. Instead, comes a bombardment of images as if she is somewhere else entirely, a whole new reality moving around her.

The forest is unfamiliar. In fact, everything is unfamiliar. How did she get here? Where was she before this? Such simple, usual details escape Wren as she spins around to take stock of the thick-trunked, dense trees surrounding her.

Wren is sure she was somewhere else, doing something else, but everything in her recent memory is blurred like the fog rolling over the forest floor.

"Help!"

It's coming from up ahead. Without thinking, Wren launches forward, swerving around the trees with ease. The call comes again, and once Wren pushes a little further, she sees its owner.

A man, his violet hair tied in a messy bun with strands falling in front of his terrified face and around his pointed ears. Someone of elven blood. The tall, antlered figure dragging him by the back of his shirt, however, is distinctly unlike any mortal being Wren has ever seen.

"Stop!" Wren calls out. "Where are you taking him?"

The tall figure stops and turns. It looks at her with eyes of pitch black, its long hair so many odd hues of muted, metallic colour that shift with any movement. Its skin is pure silver.

"Wherever I please," it says, voice low and raspy.

Wren draws her sword. "Put him down."

It tilts its head, its too large mouth curling on one side in a smile. "... no."

The uncaring, smug cadence of the single word turns Wren's blood to ice. She braces herself to charge. But before she can even launch herself off the balls of her feet, her entire body locks in place. The fey creature—that must be what it is, to be full of such strange colour that hurts Wren's eyes to even look at—has its free hand raised, holding her still across the twenty foot distance.

"I'll not release my prize without a worthy exchange," it says. "And you will not release him by force."

It's not a threat. It's fact, stated plain.

"What kind of exchange?" Wren asks. "I don't have any money. Not enough, anyway."

The fey creature makes an odd noise. A laugh, perhaps. "I did not say money. I said worth. What worth would I place on dead, cold metal? But sentiment... sacrifice... those can be delicious."

Wren tries to get her mind around what it is saying, and struggles. "I—I'm still not sure I have anything."

"You place value on his life. So what do you have, of value?"

Nothing. Nothing which is valuable to anyone but her, anyway. Only her armour and her sword.

Sentiment. And sacrifice.

Her heart rebels the moment it catches up to her mind. No. Surely not. And yet... there is nothing else that makes sense.

"This sword is my father's," she says, closing her eyes as tears spring to their corners. "It's the most precious thing I have. Is that a worthy trade?"

"*... yes.*"

Wren comes back to the world, trembling. The gem's bright colour is the first thing that strikes her, and as her vision clears everything she could not remember while in the trial's vision comes rushing back, along with the trial itself.

Her shaking hand reaches behind her for the handle of her sword, and when it closes around the familiar shape, she nearly bursts into tears.

"*Fuck*," she whispers, shaking her head. "*Fuck* that."

"Wren," Reverie says from next to her, concerned. But there isn't time for such things now.

"Lark, we're through," Wren calls behind them, astounded she even remembers to say it before she grabs Reverie and pulls her past the gem and into the next passage.

They run. Glances back show only chaos and twisting metal, while their ears are filled with shouts from Lark and Nightingale both, mixing with the snake's discordance in a horrid orchestration. All too quickly, the only thing visible behind them is stone as they turn corners, and after ten seconds the sound vanishes entirely.

"Fuck," Wren says, slowing down and letting everything wash over her. "*Fuck*!" She kicks a wall and gets to add her furious toe to the list of today's problems.

"I'm sure they'll be okay." It's one of the least convincing things Reverie has ever said.

Wren shakes her head. "Physically, *maybe*, if that snake doesn't rip them apart. But it's not that simple. I don't know what happens if she gets to... their heart."

"What do you mean? Like… you're worried Lark is going to switch sides? Or just… break?" Reverie almost whispers the last part.

Instead of pacing, Wren forces herself to keep a strong stride moving forward, towards the next trial. "They *love* her. Still. Despite everything. They can't help it, and they can't bring themself to hurt her… the hold she still has on them is terrifying."

Reverie curses. "So that talk about love…"

"Yeah."

"I *knew* it sounded messy."

"They've been putting on a brave face, but I saw them in Kequm, when they found out she was out, when they saw her again—" Wren takes a long breath in and out to calm herself. It does little. "This is so hard for them. And we have to help Lark, but we can't let that mean helping Nightingale, and I *need* someone else to know, because I don't know if Lark sees it, I really don't."

Reverie's eyes are wide pools of gold, absorbing everything, and then she nods as she keeps pace with Wren, her shorter legs making quicker strides. "Lark's lucky to have you, and I'll do *everything* I can to help both of you."

Wren feels several emotions—worry, determination, and frustration—battle in her chest. Her torso shudders with the conflict. The care she feels for Lark beats them all down, keeping her priorities fixed. But then, love isn't exactly an emotion, is it? It might have feelings that come with it, or even drive it, love for another person is more like an oath.

"Thanks," Wren says. "That looks like the next trial. You're up."

Chapter 5

As the situation stands, Lark can either watch Nightingale teleport in circles around the creature until she runs out of magic and gets promptly eviscerated, or find a way to assist her in dispatching the fascinating thing. Both options present problems, emotional or moral, to say nothing of the physical peril involved. Lark has already shown Nightingale far more mercy than she has ever deserved. The world would no doubt be a safer place without her in it, and yet Lark can never abide the thought of letting her perish, her brilliant mind or unconquerable spirit.

The serpent flings Nightingale off its head, and Lark cannot help but wince in anticipation of an awful landing before she teleports to avoid the worst of gravity's punishment. She does, however, land wrong and crumble onto one knee.

Would I be the real monster, if I saved her?

Can I let her die in front of me?

When put as simply as that, there is little question. It is a truth Lark must acknowledge, that while it may have ramifications beyond belief, they will never be able to stand by and watch her be killed. Not while there are questions left unanswered, and emotions burning in their chest, the painful and stubborn embers in existence refusing to be blown out by the winds of change.

"Sorry," Lark says to the Scholar, before they leap at the serpent and begin climbing its neck to distract it from trying to bite Nightingale's leg off.

"What's that going to achieve?" Nightingale asks, as she scrambles to her feet.

"Once again, I find myself asking 'should I let it tear you to shreds'?"

The snake takes that as a suggestion, and lunges for Nightingale only to get another near miss. So, instead, it jerks its head and Lark goes flying. Their back hits the uncompromising stone, the wind knocked from them, with questions of sanity and sense floating around their head.

"I don't know what you think your magic is going to do against a magical construct—" Nightingale calls to them, before appearing next to them another snake bite and teleport later.

"About as good as your broken quill, or *your* magic, I'd imagine," Lark retorts, and takes her offered hand up without thinking about it. "So let's—"

They truly miss being able to curse without having to direct it to anyone in particular. Instead they can only fall when the snake's tail sweeps them right off their feet before they have even gotten comfortably vertical.

Nightingale mostly jumps over it, but has to turn it into a roll to the ground when her feet don't quite clear the top. They end up next to each other on the ground as if it is a forever destined location for them as a pair.

"*What do we know*?!" Lark demands, their voice cracking as their body begins to protest at the sheer number of bruises it is gathering with no reprieve in sight.

"Old Empire," Nightingale says, almost automatically, as she makes a portal in the floor ahead of her and comes out to the snake's right side, opposite the mysterious entryway, where Lark had been when it first emerged. "Magic. Metal. Non-sentient."

Lark gets a moment to breathe thanks to her location shift, as the snake is still focused on her. "And thus immune to both of our magics—" Pause as they lose sight of her when the serpent twists and charges, forcing out another teleport. "It's been here for centuries. Something's sustaining it—"

Another tail swipe in Lark's direction. This time they are ready to jump over it, but forget about the wall on the other side and slam into it with a wince.

"Magic power source, or mechanical?" Nightingale asks from the other side of the construct.

"Mechanical's unlikely to still be in working order after all this time," Lark says as they find her face again.

They should really be sticking together. Nightingale can't watch the snake while Lark is speaking, because Lark needs her eyes. As such, they miss the early indicators, the way the snake has reared back to prepare for the biggest lunge yet.

It springs like a loose coil, and the only thing Lark sees is Nightingale leaping *right into its mouth* and Lark cannot even scream her name but their heart drops through their stomach like a plummeting boulder.

Then, a portal opens in front of them and Nightingale tumbles out with two metal fangs stuck in her arm.

"Oh," Lark breathes. It's awful how relieved they sound, how it makes her smile through the pain. She is standing with all of her weight on the uninjured leg, and she'd never let her face betray weakness but her breathing does.

They glance at the snake, which is doing its best to turn around in the restrictive corridor, and Lark knows they have seconds.

"Scholar, I'm sorry, I need her alive," Lark prays, and perhaps they meant to say *we*. They put their hand over the worst wound in Nightingale's arm, yanking out the metal with their other hand and soothing the area with golden magic. The magic flows as easily as any time, bringing new questions about the Scholar's given magic in Lark's hands. Is it trust? Is it more power in the hands of the wielder than Lark thought? Is the magic not just Gifted but entrusted?

Is Lark even worthy of such a thing?

"Forgot how good that feels," Nightingale murmurs, as she shifts to stand between Lark and the serpent, making it impossible for Lark to say *we need a plan*.

They're still too close together, and Lark's entire body feels muted and exhausted, no longer sure how to react to save itself—

Nightingale grabs Lark by the shirt as the snake lunges again, and takes Lark for their first plus one portal ride. For a fleeting moment, they are somewhere else entirely, a place of pure darkness, and when Lark shouts no new air fills their lungs. As they appear in the corridor twenty feet back down towards the first trial gate, they gasp desperately for oxygen.

Nightingale hits the wall. Lark slams into her, bumping her glasses eschew. Without thinking, Lark reaches up to adjust them, as they *have* so many times in the past. Nightingale is dead still. Usually that would signal something dangerous, an act of violence incoming. But her pupils are dilated and for the first time in a long time, a soft pulse of gold and blue escapes into her aura. Her genuine surprise, betrayed.

"I—ahem. There," Lark says, cursing their traitorous hands and treacherous heart and every inch of them refusing to remember she is the enemy now, not a friend or anything close.

"Thank you," Nightingale exhales. For once, her voice is devoid of sarcasm. Her eyes glance left, to the approaching creature. "Ready to go again?" Lark cannot actually answer. "Oh, and hold your breath this time. Forgot to say."

This time she pushes them instead of pulls, and the pair go through another portal to avoid the next attack. The same darkness flashes past Lark's eyes before they come out the other side.

"What the *fuck* is that place?!" Lark demands, when they can once again gulp in air.

Nightingale shrugs, because answering the question would only be helpful, and her smile is breathless and beautiful and completely ill-suited to the current crisis. But she has always been one to smile where she oughtn't.

"This is almost like dancing," she says, voice soft.

"Oh, so that's why I hate it," Lark retorts.

"I could do this all day."

"No, you couldn't, you'll run out of magic soon—"

Another lunge. Another teleport. They end up as close to the trial as Nightingale's sight could see. This time, Nightingale laughs, a peeling sound of whimsy echoing against the stone.

"Shall we rip it open and see what's powering it?" Nightingale asks.

It's difficult to focus when one is consistently being yanked through what might be an entirely different plane of existence. Lark can only stare at her. "With *what*?"

"I have a broken quill and a stubborn disposition, so it doesn't have a chance," she chuckles. "So long as you can get on its head and cause some problems."

"Just a minor conditional!" Lark squeaks. And yet, what choice do they have? They cannot even pretend to refuse her.

The teleports are doing a marvellous job of wasting the snake's time, but Lark has no doubt that its energy will be near infinite, and with every leap Nightingale is less steady. They're dead meat if no portal opens because Nightingale has burned through her reserve or simply collapsed.

There is a certain pool of power each mage possesses, in the case of Innate and Gifted mages. The magic physically tied to an Innate mage, or being channeled by a Gifted mage. It can tire a body, after a while, like anything else. (Disciplined mages take more of a mental tax, but the intricacy of their magic tends to make it harder for them to burn through it quickly.) Once one's initial limit has been reached, it's certainly possible to push your body to channel more, and more... but only for so long, and it is certainly only for emergencies.

Nightingale grins as if they're having a small disagreement in a market. "Darling, I'd never ask anything of you outside your ability. You have more dumb luck than anyone else I know—"

"For fuck's sake—get me above it then," Lark says.

Her portal and smile flash in the same moment, and then they are falling on top of a scaly head. Nightingale rolls off the side into a new portal, and comes out at the ground, right in front of the damned serpent.

It lunges. Nightingale dives, slides, managing to get right underneath the head. From there Lark loses sight of her, but there is an awful whine of metal on metal. The snake snarls and twists, but with both of its enemies in places it cannot reach, there is little it can do.

"Got an opening," Nightingale says, voice laboured. "Just keep—"

Unfortunately, little is not the same as nothing. The snake finds two courses of action left to it and undertakes both simultaneously.

It surges forward, crushing Nightingale under its large belly, and charges into the wall to its right, twisting its head so Lark has no choice but to leap for the ground if they do not want to greet the wall violently.

It's not a dignified landing. Lark can only jump to their feet and avoid looking at where Nightingale had vanished beneath it, for fear of seeing something that will distract them from the necessary action.

The hole in the metal is there, in the closest equivalent the thing has to a neck, and if Lark wants to get out of this alive they need to make it bigger and find the power core. With a prayer of protection to cover themself, they unceremoniously yank at it with the hand not clutching their amulet.

"Protect me so that I might find this hidden power and knowledge, and use it for good, shield me from the bite of metal, protect me..."

The metal is deadly sharp. Lark feels it slice their skin, but not as deeply as it would have without the magic creating a thin barrier of resistance. It's blood, though. Still enough of a concern to have Lark curse and get their long sleeve to cover the hand before they return to the arduous task. They yank with every bit of mediocre strength they possess for any give in the metal, to get another inch open.

The serpent twists and tries to get a better angle to snap at Lark, while Lark does everything they can to follow its movements, to stay in the zone where its teeth cannot reach but ready to move if it tries to repeat what it did to Nightingale.

One big yank, and something bright shines from within. A core gleaming with magic. A core Lark needs to destroy. The problem is that magic can fortify mundane materials, and it's impossible to know how durable any given magical thing is until... well, you attack it.

"Here goes something," Lark says to the Scholar, hoping he appreciates the scientific endeavour as they take a boom ball from their pocket and throw it into the core.

Magic can be a bit like chemistry. A dormant ingredient can become wildly active when it meets something else. This had been obvious in the Collection where they had met Reverie, where a hundred and one magical things had only been able to coexist in harmony due to a meticulous floorplan created by its curator. Two objects had been switched, and a terrifying entity had been unleashed.

In this particular case, however, a magical power core gets to meet a metallic ball designed to implode with the force of a thundercrack.

In hindsight, maybe Lark should have guessed how bright the explosion might be, but all they can do is bring their arm to cover their assaulted eyes. After it comes a small cracking sound, then another, and when Lark hazards a glance they see the core pulsing, the flashes accelerating in perfect time with odd drones—

Oh no.

Lark will be lucky if they have seconds. They dive for the ground where Nightingale is trapped, gasping out their quickest prayer of protection to wrap them both in a shield in the instant before the entire snake explodes.

When Nightingale had collapsed a building on top of Lark and Wren with an arcane explosion, Lark's magical shielding had saved them, and held long enough for Wren to shift some rubble to buy them breathing room.

This is magical force condensed into an implosion of a single instant. It obliterates Lark's shield, and the world vanishes.

The world vanishes.

Chapter 6

Pain is the first thing to come back. Aches in every inch of Lark's body, a tingling on the back of their neck, and they are unsure if bones can be bruised but it certainly *feels* as if it's possible. Even lifting their head to survey the situation is an ordeal.

Good news: Lark doesn't need to somehow get Nightingale out from under the snake, as the snake no longer exists. There is only metal, half melted and scattered in shrapnel across the floor.

Bad news: Nightingale is splayed and still.

Lark tries to say her name, to urge her to move, and of course they cannot. Her name spends more time on their tongue than any other, on any day, always mocking Lark that they cannot utter it for her absence or else the judgement of another.

With an apology they can only think, Lark pinches Nightingale in the shoulder. A noise escapes her, one of exhausted protest, and the relief that Lark feels might as well be poison for the good it will do them in the end.

Their head pounds, and heart stutters, and there is only energy to lie next to her and let their body come to terms with the shock it has suffered. It is setting in now, the world blurring and every inch of them feeling hot and cold and itchy.

Lying next to Nightingale with one's guard entirely down is of course not the smart thing to do. Her broken quill is still perfectly apt as far as weapons go. She could smother Lark with her magic, or disarm them with the right choice of words and those endless, impossible eyes. But after they have put so much effort into saving her life, they will take the risk of giving her the benefit of the doubt. Of hoping that whatever lingers between them means just enough that she will let them have a few moments of quiet.

In the dim, flickering light of the braziers, the silence is punctuated only by their laboured breaths and a deafening absence of violence. It's the closest to peace that Lark has felt all week.

It's hard to say how much time passes, but eventually Lark turns their head and finds their eyes caught in pools of lilac.

"Hello," they whisper, and curse themself the moment they do.

Nightingale exhales. "Hello."

As if by unspoken agreement, they both sit up and groan at the effort involved. It leaves them upright and opposite, like they had been in Kequm, with a building burning around them. Lark had been unprepared, unaware of how powerfully affected they would be by her proximity. This time, they are painfully aware of their shortcomings.

It doesn't make being this close to Nightingale easy. She has no right to be so beautiful while so wrecked. Her hair is tangled, her face covered in scrapes (Lark imagines they look no better). Her hand travels across her ribs and elicits a wince.

"Broken?" Lark asks.

"Think so." Nightingale makes another face. "Getting crushed by a huge construct? Not an activity I recommend."

"Noted." Lark puts their hand over hers and murmurs another prayer. It is easier to focus on helping, than marvel at her. Beauty and unresolved emotions or not, they have a mission. Questions to get answers to. Direction and purpose where previously they were drowning in doubts and disorientation.

Their prayer is the same they uttered in the head of their skirmish, an apology and a plea all at once, driven purely by the fact that no one deserves suffering when it can be halted. Not even Nightingale. Suffering achieves nothing.

The magic bleeds from them into her, and she exhales long and slow. It had been a commonplace thing between them, once. They had always been a pair to enable each other's recklessness. And yet, now the healing itself feels far more reckless than anything previously undertaken. It feels like so much more than magic. Questions. Longing. Connection.

Intimacy is a dangerous thing. People talk of it as if it's soft, but Lark knows better now. It is a jagged thing, ready to cut you the moment you misstep. It's a precipice leading to either a great unknown or a terrible familiarity. This space between Lark and

Nightingale is miniscule, and at the point of contact where their hands touch, nonexistent.

Lark pulls away as the prayer finishes, and it still feels too late.

"Your glasses," they say. The lenses are cracked, but not shattered. A small mercy.

Nightingale sighs. "I'll manage. This is the real bitch." She holds up her right hand, where the broken quill still stands proud in its small harness at the edge of her sleeve. For the first time that Lark has seen in an age, worry etches itself across her face. Her fingers twitch as her eyes dart to the scattered remains of the construct.

Lark remembers what being without a writing implement can do to her. The way she had nearly torn their backpacks apart looking for quill and paper to document the phenomenon of Lark not being able to speak if they weren't looking at her; their new reality, laid out before them, not entirely understood yet.

"Here," Lark says, handing her a piece of charcoal from one of their pockets. "That should work for now."

Nightingale all but snatches it. There is no verbal gratitude, but her eyes scream it as her right hand flies into action across the grime-smeared notepad strapped to her leg.

"So... now what?" she asks. A moment after she speaks the question, her back straightens and neck tenses, perhaps now belatedly remembering the nature of their current acquaintance.

"I'm supposed to be capturing you," Lark says, to put the line clearly in the sand.

Nightingale snorts. "How's that working out for you?"

"Well, I can't capture you if you're dead, so saving your life is a good start."

"Obviously, but—" She stops, her smile slipping. "You could have tied me up while I was out. Why didn't you?"

Lark wants to scream. Not at her, but at themself, for not thinking of that for a single moment. The obvious course of action had been obscured by the desperate need to help her. Pathetic. It is everything they can do to keep their face as stoic as possible, and they have no idea if they succeed.

"You're not going to trick me into explaining myself to you," Lark sniffs. "I don't owe you anything."

"Debatable." Nightingale stands and scans the area. "Gods' tits, is it *putting itself back together*?"

Lark follows her gaze and is horrified to see the scraps of metal inching towards a central point where the largest part of the remains lies.

"Scholar preserve us," Lark curses. "We can't stay here."

"Of course we're not *staying here*." Nightingale continues looking around, and heads for the mysterious area of wall the snake had come in through. It's still shimmering. "I tried to go through this when I failed the trial. I could feel that it isn't a wall, but it wouldn't let me through. That snake came through it, though, so I wonder..."

When she reaches it, her hand passes through as if nothing were there at all.

"Seems to be open now. Good. We might be able to use it to get to other parts of the labyrinth."

"Wren touched it, and it was just stone," Lark says as they come over to see for themself. Their hand goes through it too.

"Wren isn't like us," Nightingale murmurs, and it occurs to Lark that it's the first time she's uttered Wren's name and not used a mocking moniker. Her voice is so soft, when scorn isn't discolouring it. "Does she see the stars?"

"She does. At the full moon." The stars that Lark and Nightingale see every evening, the green sparkles sprawled across the sky.

"Mmm." It's impossible to know what Nightingale is thinking. "So she doesn't see the second moon, then."

At first it had just been the stars. They knew some people started seeing the band of green, if they were well-travelled. For Lark and Nightingale, they are there every night since their new abilities and odd curses had set in. But then the full moon arrived, and there had been something else. A new thing in the sky entirely, an outline not too far from the moon they had always known. A second celestial object, impossible to quantify. They had quickly learned not to speak of it to others, for fear of incredulous reactions.

"Do you know what it *means*?" Lark asks. After seeing the puppeteer in the Collection when no one else could, they are more desperate than ever for answers.

"It means that the world shifted for us," Nightingale says, and her eyes blaze with something that catches Lark's breath in their throat. "It's showing us things, letting us into its secrets. This wall is proof of what I've always suspected. Now, shall we race your friends to the centre, or not?"

The moment shatters easily enough, at *that*.

"You're assuming I'm going anywhere with you," Lark says. They cross their arms over their chest and try to use it as armour to protect their racing heart.

Nightingale tilts her head, a single eyebrow lifting. "Well, how else are you supposed to try and capture me?"

It is not unlike staring into the eyes of a real snake, with venom glinting off her fangs, inviting one to come for a leisurely walk. Lark swallows.

The last thing they want to do is agree with her, or help her. But they need to either stop her, which involves having an opportunity to do so, or at the very least keep watch on her so that she doesn't just charge ahead and kill Wren and Reverie as soon as she gets the chance.

Lark achieves nothing by staying behind.

"Very well," they say, coughing to gasp in more oxygen. "After you."

Chapter 7

THE HIDDEN PASSAGE IS made of the same stone as the main passages, but is three quarters of the size and lacks braziers—the exact size to be a bespoke route for the construct and nothing else. Nightingale walks in front, with Lark behind.

Creating light as a Gifted mage is a curious thing. With only being able to affect people directly and not the environment, the light that Lark conjures for themself and Nightingale is more like a filter over their senses, as it would be invisible to any third party. It works, and that is what matters.

Once comfortable that Nightingale is more focused on what is ahead, Lark clutches their amulet and murmurs a prayer as softly as they can. If it works, it will bind her in place. It failed in Kequm. Lark can only hope they get lucky now, since she claimed resistance to magic designed to control her. It is impossible to know how much truth was behind those words.

The spell finishes, and her body goes rigid, locked in a half-step. Lark chokes out a laugh of disbelief—but then Nightingale's leg wobbles and hits the ground, and they realise the spell never took hold.

Their exhaustion is so immense that they are not prepared for how Nightingale twists around and throws herself at them, shoving them into the stone with a crack and a yelp. Their eyes meet furious lilac.

"You're more desperate than I thought," she breathes, half an inch from their face. Her breathing is shallow from exertion. "I'll say it again, to save us both time and energy we don't have. I'm. Protected. If you want to disable me, you'll have to do it the old-fashioned way."

"Who's giving you power *and* protection?" Lark asks, bewildered. "Most of us don't get both, so what are you—"

"*Who* isn't the word I would use," Nightingale snorts. "And that's my business."

Lark can only gape at her. "That darkness you leap through, Nightingale—if you've made some pact with a creature of the Abyss, if I have to go down there and save your bloody soul one day, Nightingale, I swear—"

"Save my soul?" Her voice is so soft it's barely audible. Her head tilted, something in her eyes searching so deep within Lark's face they can almost feel prying claws trying to tear them open from the inside out. "Would you really?"

"What the *fuck* do you think I've been trying to do, all this time?" Lark asks. Tears sting their eyes, absolutely without their permission.

Nightingale swallows. Her hands tighten on their shoulders, biting their skin even through double layers of fabric. "Are you trying to save me? Or change me?"

She gives them no chance to answer. The moment the words have left her mouth, she steps backward into a portal which takes her several feet ahead down the passage. Lark stares after her and wipes their coat sleeves against their wet eyes.

If their body could get its act together so they can survive the day, that would be marvellous.

CHAPTER 7

They walk. Lark scrambles for inspiration, for something. A way to stop her that won't backfire. But every failed attempt increases the chances of Reverie or Wren meeting their end at Nightingale's hands, victims of her stoked ire.

Is this how Reverie feels all the time, with Ferdinand on her heels? Trying to appease him, in small ways, to avoid stoking the fires of his petulant nature? How impossible is the world that Lark is comparing Nightingale to a goose?

Usually the lack of sense of it all is a comforting thing. A delightful challenge, a thing to be explored, a meaning to be found and connections to be made. Right now, Lark has a headache and is wishing everything could be a bit simpler for a few weeks. Heck, they'd take *days* at this point.

It takes perhaps too long for Lark to realise the tunnel is sloping downward, further into the earth. Eventually it comes out into a cylindrical space with a round indent in the floor, glowing a faint green that reminds Lark of the braziers. Nine passages, not including the one they've just come from, branch out from the central space.

"Ten," Nightingale murmurs. She glances back at them. "What do you think? Ten trials?"

"Logical leap, yes," Lark says. Every part of the chamber is identical. There are no numbers, no differences in shape. The symmetry is astounding.

"So we might be able to skip to the end, if we can just—"

Just make a guess. Coming from the second passage, if they are arranged in consecutive order then one of the ones two passages over will likely lead them to the final trial. The best shortcut. Something that would take Nightingale right to her prize.

Lark wishes today's sparks of inspiration could be ones that come with more dignity. Perhaps it's the desperation getting in the way.

"Work out which one will get us to the end," they finish for her, only a second too late. They let the genuine enthusiasm of the puzzle infect their voice as they bounce up to her, hoping to keep her suspicion at bay for just a few more moments.

"Exactly," Nightingale says, and she grins before glancing away to run her eyes over the passage entrances. "So it must be—"

Lark tackles her into the central indent. They hit the hard floor and Lark grabs Nightingale by her clothes and drags her, rolls her, before she can work out what they are doing and why, and try to stop it. It is an awful scrap of flailing limbs and cursing protests, but at least this time she doesn't stab them.

"Why the fuck would you—" Nightingale stops wrestling for a moment and glances around. The dawning disorientation on her face is the sweetest triumph might hope to taste today.

Her glare, when it comes to rest on them, could wither a tree. "Alright, *darling*. Now what?"

"Now we pick one, and see where it takes us," Lark says. "No skipping to the end. I won't let you."

She clicks her tongue. "I don't need you. I could suffocate you until you pass out, and then go any way I like."

Lark doesn't feel bad for how starkly they laugh in her face. "And get stuck the moment you're asked to be a decent person, again?" Lark counters. "Let's be honest. Neither of us are likely to make it through without the other. If you want to race my friends—my friends who are kind, and brilliant, and hardworking, and a thousand other excellent things—you're going to need me to have even a *chance*."

Her silence is damning. It's delicious. It takes almost thirty seconds for her face to shift, but when it does, it takes on a smile.

"I'd forgotten what it was like to lose a match," she says. "Let alone two in a row. You're making up for Kequm, aren't you?"

"Obviously," Lark says, accepting the hand she extends to help them up. "You're taking it better than expected."

"Oh, you've just let me taste victory too much," Nightingale replies, actually chuckling. "Losing builds character."

"That's true."

"Which is why you're so remarkable, obviously."

"Hey!"

Nightingale giggles at how Lark wags an indignant finger in her direction. To make it worse, an absolutely forbidden chuckle escapes their lips, making them frown.

"No," they say, gesturing even more emphatically with aforementioned finger. "No. We are *not* having fun. Not us. Not together." *Not anymore.*

"Why not?" Nightingale says. "There's no point in us making each other more miserable than we already do. What's the point in being alive if not to seize feeling joy before it's snuffed out?"

Lark's heart jumps into their throat, and for a precious second they see her as they had years before. The most brilliant person they had ever had the pleasure to stand in the presence of, inspiring them with how she can regard the world with such wide, hungry eyes.

"Those words would be much prettier," Lark says, "if you didn't snuff out the joy of others. By killing them, because you don't care if *they're* alive."

"See?" Nightingale remarks, throwing her arms up with all derision and zero remorse. "Snuffed, right away."

So many ugly words come to Lark's tongue. They choose silence and push past Nightingale, into a corridor chosen at random. They hope with everything they have, and pray a bit more for good measure, that their choice is a passage which puts them behind Wren and Reverie.

Walking ahead of Nightingale is a questionable strategic choice. It provides the perfect opportunity for stabbing or magical disabling, but that's the problem with the two of them, isn't it? Lark is not the only one hindered by their past. Nightingale's weakness is starkly clear; she could not truly harm Lark anymore than they could harm her. (A bit of maiming, sure. That much had been made clear in Kequm. But it's not the same, when one has healing abilities which can turn such things into trivial inconveniences.)

They walk until they reach a shimmering oval in the wall, identical to how the previous one had looked from the other side. Above it, a small gem lights up when Lark steps close. Proximity-triggered magic? Working only from the interior? Is that how the snake had been able to open the passage, when Nightingale hadn't been able to beforehand, from the other side?

Lark glances over their shoulder at Nightingale, who is silently waiting for them to proceed. They look back, take a deep breath, and step through. Sure enough, they are back in the main body of the Labyrinth, with a trial wall and crystal to their right. Just like the others.

"Alright, let's see what we've got," Nightingale says as she comes in behind them. "Who's going first?"

Lark flourishes their hand towards her. "After you." A new idea has come, fast and possibly crucial, and their heartbeat has doubled in pace under the pressure of executing it at such short notice.

They wait until Nightingale puts her hand on the trial crystal, until they know the voice of the trial will be all she can perceive, and dash down the corridor to scribble a note on a scrap of paper.

Wren, Reverie, if reading, Nightingale & I ahead of you. Explain later. Be careful and clever, L

Once it has dropped from their fingers to the floor, Lark hurries back to the trial so that they are next to Nightingale when it glows and she comes back to herself. They take a moment to glance at the label for the trial. *Trial of Commitment.*

"Well done," Lark says, as their eyes come back down.

"Easy enough," Nightingale replies, shrugging. "When something is mine, I give it everything I possess."

The way she holds Lark's gaze as she says it... they nod, holding back a scream. It is simultaneously true and an atrocious joke.

I was yours, they want to say. *Until you chose something else, and gave that everything until there was nothing left for me.*

Of course, they say nothing, and their anguish swirls the darkest of blues in their vision. They wonder if it burns so hot Nightingale can feel it as she walks beside them. Neither speak a word. Perhaps because today far too many have been uttered already. Too many more may be the undoing of one or both of them.

Ahead of them, the next trial appears. Lark steps forward and tries to swallow their nerves as they read: *Trial of Honesty.*

Interlude

II - REVERIE

The matter of deeply personal trials and long walks next to a rigidly stressed Wren does not make for a light-hearted experience. The fact that they have started to encounter mangled, occasionally charred old skeletons in some of the passageways? Even worse. The laughter of the newly resummoned goose becomes the icing on the terrible cake.

While perfectly able to be serious when the situation calls for it, Reverie is beginning to worry that if she doesn't do something about the frown creasing Wren's brows, they might be stuck that way.

Perhaps it is time for something Reverie excels at: distraction.

Her lyre slides easily from its harness on her backpack, and strumming it once pulls the tension from her body like the truest sort of magic she may ever know. Like reaching for the strands of potential around her when she is casting a spell, she reaches inside herself to find words, to find the notes of a melody.

She strums four notes, hums contently, and turns it into a simple rhythm easy to repeat. The words come quickly after that; it has always felt easy to put words to notes, to let her ideas and feelings flow so freely in a way they never can otherwise.

"*Underground, deep way down,*" Reverie sings, "*far from any city.*"

Wren glances her way, an eyebrow up, but she says nothing and keeps walking.

"*Old elves were here and Lark's ex ought to be feared, but I do think she's quite sexy—*"

"Reverie, what the fuck?" Wren asks. There is too much bewilderment on her face to leave any room for worry.

"What?" Reverie asks, blinking at her innocently, continuing to strum her motif over and over.

"Are you—she tried to kill you! How can you be thinking about this?!"

"Hey, I take nearly getting killed really seriously," Reverie says. "I have to. But now that I'm still breathing and she's far away... damn. I'm just saying. I get it."

You'd fuck anything that paid you enough attention, Ferdinand says. *You're just like your grandmother.*

"Ew," Reverie says, wrinkling her nose. "No more comparing me to Ama. It's gross." And telepathically, she adds, *be quiet. I'm trying to cheer up Wren.*

The absolute lack of comprehension on Wren's face prompts a new question from Reverie.

"Do you... not like women? I thought I was picking up on some—"

"No, of course I do," Wren replies, stiffening. "You know, theoretically, if I had the time—gods, being a lesbian was the easiest thing to learn about myself. But that doesn't mean I'm attracted to *murderers* just because they're not men."

"I'd never *act* on it!" Reverie says, cackling. "I'm just saying."

"And I worry about you," Wren says. A moment later, an odd laugh wrenches itself from her throat. "You're ridiculous. I hope you know that."

Reverie giggles. A new verse has come to her. "*I never said it was a good idea, I'm a simple appreciator— of nature's work and an evil smirk, and I hope she doesn't stab me later!*"

Wren groans and buries her head in her hands. It's close enough to a laugh that victory soars through Reverie's chest. There is a reason that diverting is a synonym of entertaining. Sometimes, it is the kindest thing you can do for someone.

"*Oh Wren!*" Reverie changes the tune, tuning into a croon, a drawn out exclamation. "*You're so fiiiine.*" The note doesn't hit right on that one and she makes a face before latching onto a new rhythm for the next part, faster. "*I love how you say what's on your mind, you are far more sensible than I, I so love your lesbian mind—*"

"You just rhymed mind with mind," splutters a blushing Wren. She crosses her arms over her chest, like that will hide the scarlet that has crept up her neck, ears and cheeks.

Reverie feigns great offense with the most dramatic of exclamations and the haughtiest voice she can affect. "Then *you* make up a song for us, on the spot, oh great critic of my lyrics!"

"... I think you're joking, but just in case you're not... no."

Reverie can't hold back a grin at that, and Wren returns it a moment later, if a bit delayed.

They walk in higher spirits, with Reverie playing a selection of songs she knows, ones that are the right medium between cheering and melancholy, as too strong a feeling of either is not right for today.

It is such a pleasant, brief pocket of time in light so dim and green, that Reverie almost misses the scrap of paper on the ground ahead of them. Wren walks right past it, but the moment Ferdinand stops to poke it with his beak, Reverie bends to retrieve it from the stone. It doesn't have the same discolouration as anything near the skeletons—and none of them had paper lying next to them, only weapons long rusted.

The handwriting is unfamiliar. But the words could belong to only one person.

"Wren."

There must be something new and strained in her voice, because Wren whips around with her shoulders tense and her hand on her sword hilt. She glances around, and narrows her eyes.

"What?"

Reverie holds out the paper. "Big problem."

Wren takes it in two strides and one pluck. Her eyes scan the page, and within a moment her brow furrows. Then comes a string of colourful words, more bitter than Reverie had ever thought her capable of. But also, Reverie had not fully understood the Nightingale problem nor Wren's part in it, until today.

What? What is it? Ferdinand asks, launching himself into the air to try and get a look. *Let me see!* Reverie bats him away and mentally relays the message so he'll stop pestering Wren.

"After all that!" Wren exhales long and slow, crumpling the paper in her hand. "How is that fair?"

"Since when is life *fair*?" Reverie asks, incredulously.

Wren makes a face. It is one that speaks of belated agreement, one which was always going to come because no one could go through what Wren and her village did and be left with such an incorrect idea.

"You know what I mean," the warrior says. Her fingers try to smooth away her frown. "How are we going to stop her if she's going to get to it first?"

Reverie chews on her bottom lip thoughtfully. "So... we're assuming Lark won't stop her?"

"We can't assume anything, when it comes to her," Wren says. "But if Lark does stop her, we might not have anything to worry about. So we prepare for if they *don't*. We try to catch up. We go as fast as we can."

Reverie nods. Inappropriate delight tickles her from the inside out at the thought of a deadly countdown, of the stakes and the race. She lurches forward to the next trial.

The Trial of Commitment.

"Feeling okay about this one?" Wren asks.

"Uh," Reverie says, about as honestly as possible. Ferdinand honks just rudely enough to get a kick to his underside and a new 'shut the fuck up' command.

Commitment certainly isn't a word she's spent much time ruminating on. But a test is a test, and now there is no time to waste.

Reverie will never get used to the sensation of the trial magic touching her mind when her hand meets the crystal. It is not fear of the unknown—Reverie welcomes that. It is a connection of a stronger order, hearing without her ears a concept in two tongues. The Old Elvish, which she can half follow, and the translation coming in strong right on top of it. It's dizzying.

Strongest of all, the questions delivered are ones enchanted by people so long dead they are half mythical. When building this protection, this intricate place of guardianship, could they have imagined how long this place would stand? Did they know that the voices of the trials would be all that remained, the last voices to speak for them?

How lucky she is to touch the past like this. How unlucky she is that it is here to pass judgement on her.

What does it mean to you, to commit to something or someone?

Reverie almost laughs. However she had expected the question to be phrased, this comes as a surprise. She has never needed to commit to her family—that would imply choice, or an ability to argue with destiny, which apparently one is not allowed to do no matter how obvious the error is. She has only ever been in love in a young fancy, something fated to never be. The only other two she has been involved with romantically had been too in love with each other to require anything but fun from her.

Which is fine. Real love must involve honesty, anyone with sense must know, and if Reverie were to ever supply that, no relationship would endure.

But there is one aspect of her life that shines through. One commitment. Something that doesn't care how awful she is, or how trapped she might be by her family legacy.

The stage. Stories, coming to life with words and tune and movement, the way Reverie devours every script and score until she knows it by heart. Diving into the details of what makes a character tick until everything about them is second nature. Her chest and how it aches with real pain over pure fiction, because while she is on the stage, in their head, it is real to her.

Commitment is where belief meets action, she thinks as her answer. *It's believing something to have meaning and truth, and taking every step to make it shine as bright as possible. It's giving everything because of what you feel, and knowing no obstacle will be enough to keep you from it.*

The gem warms. Reverie lingers for a moment longer, caught in a fanciful vision of herself on a grand stage, in a theatre for the masses. Singing her heart out. Dancing with everything she has. Bringing herself and the crowd to tears.

A future stolen. The future she *will* find her way back to, if she doesn't die first.

Chapter 8

Is Lark an honest person? They've never thought about it for any extended period of time. They are not one for lies, generally, but is withholding the truth not similarly dishonest? There are many truths Lark keeps folded beneath their tongue.

One way or another, it is time to find out. Lark inhales slowly and puts their hand on the gem, pointedly ignoring the weighted gaze of Nightingale behind them.

Give the answer to the question, as honestly as possible, and ensure you believe it with all of your heart and mind.

Lark's heart kicks up at the wording. It's more pressure than they expected, and they had never doubted their own conviction as much as they have this week, or believed in themself so little. But they cannot stop the question from coming.

What would you give your life for?

Slow exhale. No panic. Just think. Just be rational. Not an easy question, to be sure, but it was never going to be. They are not one for sacrifices; they are too scared, too selfish, too clever to not find a workaround.

Perhaps that is not even their fault. Before coming to the Scholar's university in Kequm, being raised at Myron Manor by a collective of extraordinarily clever people had taught Lark to prioritise knowledge and brilliance and progress above all else. The collective had once banded together to weave a horrendous lie to preserve their institution, all because of the belief that they were worth preserving at almost any cost. Not a normal upbringing, not one that accepts defeat easily.

Would they give their life for one of their friends? Perhaps, but even the slightest feeling of hesitation warns them against answering that way. Shame floods in hot and fast at *that*.

An honest answer could be simply... nothing. But what would Lark be, if there was nothing they valued more than their own life? How pathetic, how small could they be, for that to be the most honest answer they could give?

They didn't want to be small. They didn't want to fade into nothing, as they would if that were all they could stand for. So what did they want? To be a hero? They have their moments of helpfulness, but they pale in comparison even to their own travelling group.

What would be big enough for them? A worthwhile trade, for their half-lifetime of skills and work and study?

Memories come hard and fast of the declaration attack on Kequm where the dragons had opened war on the Theocracy. Lark had not been present, but had rushed there in the aftermath. A Disciplined mage who had witnessed it all had managed to transform their memories into pictures which played out for anyone to see, stored in a book given to the Scholar's archive.

Fire everywhere. People running, silent screams leaving their mouths. Innocents without power suffering at the hands of those who misuse the power they possess.

One honest answer becomes starkly clear.

I would give my life to end the war today, if I could.

And then they wait, in agony, steeling themself against doubt because for once in their life they need to be sure about *themself* and not someone else. And yet, somehow that is the hardest thing of all.

The gem pulses warm under Lark's hand. They open their eyes to see the wall faded to nothing.

"Very good," Nightingale says from behind them, as she comes to stand with them.

Lark shrugs, even as they release a long breath and try to push away all thoughts of sacrifice for a day that hopefully will never come.. "I suppose the next one is yours to take, whatever it is."

"If that thing comes back for round two because we get it wrong—" Nightingale mutters. Lark refrains from pointing out that they are quite certain the snake is coming for her regardless of additional failures. Constructs with such specific instructions are difficult to dissuade. Even the thought of facing it again makes them want to cry with exhaustion. Only the importance of what lies ahead keeps them moving forward with how their battered body protests every step.

Shattered pieces of bone cover the next passage. Lark tracks them, categorises them, arranging them into full skeletal structures in their head to get an estimate at the number. At least ten femurs. Six skulls. A dozen kneecaps. Six dead minimum, then. It all makes sense when they reach the sign which reads '*Trial of Humility*'.

"Ah," Lark says. They look at Nightingale with a raised eyebrow.

She rolls her eyes, and puts her hand on the crystal because she must. Her eyes close. A frown turns her lips, and then a loud noise rings out through the corridor, echoing through the stone and Lark's already pounding head.

"Yeah, fuck you too," Nightingale says to the gem. She looks at Lark. "Now what?"

"Er," Lark says, intelligently. "Well. Regenerating snake presents a problem. Time may still be on our side. *But* if this place relies on its sentinel to dispatch unworthy groups, it must reset for the new group. The question is, how long? It could go by the day, the hour—but that thing could destroy most in much less time than that, especially with that self-destruct fail-safe."

"Your friends got through about five minutes after I failed," Nightingale considers. "So... five minutes or less."

Lark puts their hand on the gem. It's cold. They keep it there, for when something changes.

"You'll be able to pass," Nightingale says. "But it isn't a point in your favour. You never *have* given yourself enough credit."

An odd compliment, wrapped in a cryptic teaser, trying to be an insult. Things could never be simple between them, could it?

Lark does not give her the satisfaction of an answer, and focuses on the gem while counting the seconds to determine the length of the reset delay.

The gem warms after four minutes and forty two seconds, meaning it is indeed five minutes total by Lark's estimate.

The trial question blazes through their mind. *Who will always outshine your greatest achievement, no matter what you do?*

A bizarre, awful laugh shakes Lark's body. A matter of humility, and Lark's answer is the woman who failed it.

Nightingale will always be a greater true seeker of knowledge than I could ever hope to be.

They have no doubt of the statement's truth, of their own belief in it. It's the closest they will ever come to admitting the tiniest part of them envies her freedom. Her ability to pursue anything she wishes to, with any method available to her. It is a forbidden thing they'll never speak aloud. But there is no lying to the trial—and is it honesty if it is silent, spoken only to something who cannot tell the secret? A deeper question, probably, than the trial cares about.

The wall fades. Lark can feel Nightingale's eyes burning into them, but they cannot bear to look at her. They might cry, or fall into her arms, or confess a thousand admirations which must never pass their lips. To avoid such atrocities they can only walk onward.

She catches up quickly enough, and when they glance over against their better instincts, she is shifting her gaze away a moment too late.

More walking. More almost talking but not quite, almost looking at each other. More heaviness in Lark's head and hands and heart. More prayers that they'll get through this sane and without shackling regret.

The dank darkness of the corridors does little to brighten Lark's mood. They miss the sun, the fresh air, things they sometimes forget to appreciate at all but now want desperately. The brazier's light do little to make the place feel alive.

Two skeletons on this walk, leading up to the Trial of Conviction. Once they're close enough to read the sign, Nightingale strides forward and slams her hand onto the crystal.

It is two seconds before the wall disappears. Nightingale hums, pleased, and turns around to give Lark a mock curtsy. Lark nods in return. Of course she passed this one with flying colours. There is no snide comment to give, only stark relief it hadn't been their trial to attempt. If the last week has proven anything, it's that their conviction is lacking when it counts.

Three skeletons in the next corridor. The sign reads '*The Trial of Unbreakable Bond*'. Nightingale's frown at it perfectly encapsulates Lark's own bemusement at what it could possibly test.

"Go on, then," Nightingale says, lifting an eyebrow.

There is little to do but to put their hand down and see what happens.

Our tethers to those who walk this world with us are what give us perspective and balance. You may pass if you possess a bond with someone else, strong enough that it will be broken only by death.

Lark yanks their hand away as if the question itself is an open flame and finds themself trapped in Nightingale's eyes.

Chapter 9

Lark doesn't want to know. It's the last thing they want or need to think about, and yet they cannot keep their eyes from Nightingale's inquiring gaze. The air has left their body, surely, because there is no other way to explain how wrong everything feels.

"What was *that*?" Nightingale touches the gem. "Urgh. It won't work for me until you're done one way or another. What *is* that face you're making?"

"I—" What could Lark possibly say that isn't an outright lie she'll see through in a moment? But how can they tell the truth? If they were everything they ought to be, everything they try to be, this would not be what it is. Their answer would be different.

But, as Lark had told Reverie, mortal hearts are not so easily controlled.

"What good does waiting do? Pass or fail, get on with it," Nightingale says, crossing her arms as she leans against the trial wall. "If you're not going to explain what *unbreakable bond* means—"

"A bond broken only by death," Lark chokes out. Nightingale cocks her head, eyes narrowing. "It wants to know if I have a bond with someone that's strong enough only death could break it."

"I see," she says, voice all at once much more careful, much more slow. "And? Do you?"

Denial seems pointless, after that. Admitting to the trial is easier than admitting it to Nightingale. Even as tears prick their eyes, they put their hand back on the gem and think of her. Her name, her face, and the reality that so long as they both breathe, there will be a tether between them which cannot be severed. Whether they like it or not.

The gem pulses warm, and in Lark's periphery the wall melts away, leaving Nightingale to stumble as she loses her support. She catches herself, and her eyes find Lark's by pure magnetism. Whatever she sees in Lark's face shifts hers, and a watery sheen glosses her eyes beneath the lens of her grimy glasses.

"Oh," she whispers.

"Yes, well," Lark says, just as soft. They adjust their coat lapels with both hands as an excuse to look away from her for a momentary reprieve. They breathe in, then out. When they look up again, she is still staring. "I wish... it meant something. But that's proving rather impossible."

"Don't be silly," Nightingale says, voice thick. "Of course it means something. It just doesn't change anything."

On that at least, they can agree. Lark nods, only to start and jump back when Nightingale's hand tries to reach out toward them. The recoil is violent, as is the mirror that comes a moment later, as Nightingale snatches back her hand and charges down the open passage. Being turned away does little to hide how her sleeve comes up to wipe at her eyes under the glasses.

Until now, Kequm had been two of the worst days of Lark's life. Now, Lark would give anything for the worst thing to be a moderate stabbing to the chest. This is so, so much worse. They can barely breathe for wanting to run after her and fall into her arms, or seize her by them and scream in her face until she remembers how to be a person again.

Lark's legs stride furiously forward. It closes the gap between them too quickly and they come to a stop, to let Nightingale get ahead, before following again.

They make it about a minute before Nightingale stops and turns on her heel. The tears are gone, and now tension locks her frame, something defensive and violent in her jaw.

"What?" she asks.

"Don't," Lark warns.

"No, let's," she says with a snarl. "You're walking like you're ready to finally get payback. So, out with it."

Her eyes flash with powerful condemnation; the last thing Lark should do is give her what she wants. But actually? Lark is tired. Lark is hurt. And Lark might love her endlessly, but they are not sure they can ever, ever forgive her.

"I would have done almost anything you could have asked of me," Lark says. "And all you had to do is not kill people for your own greed. For a shortcut. And you couldn't do that, for me if no one else."

"It's not a shortcut when there's no text that holds the information," Nightingale retorts. "Sometimes someone's head is all there is. I'd *love* to take it from the living, but I can't, darling. We got the hands we got."

"You can, it's called *having a conversation*!"

"People don't spill their *best secrets* in *conversation*—"

"Perhaps not, but no one is forcing you to take the information one way or another!"

Nightingale huffs and runs a hand through her hair. "No. But I decided a long time ago I wouldn't deny myself what I want, after so many years of it never being enough."

"*That's* your excuse?" Lark laughs, hollow and horrified. "Your parents disagreed with your field of study and liked your sister better, so you're going to do what you want with no care for anyone else for the rest of your life?"

"Trivialise it all you like," she snaps. "It's too late to change my mind. About any of it."

"I know," Lark says, gesturing up and down her person as their body shakes. It might be laughter, it might be fury; they are too muddled to have any idea. "And that's what makes this all so absurd. You are so *sure* I'll never beat you, but you refuse to change. That makes it very simple."

A smirk curls across Nightingale's lips. "You sure keep saying things like that. The things you *do*, however, say something very different. You could never actually—"

She yelps as Lark lurches forward and seizes her by her jacket and shoves her into the wall of the passage.

"There are moments when this feels like the hardest thing in the world," Lark seethes. Their face is an inch from hers now, their knuckles white where they are fisted in ornate fabric between their bodies. "And then you talk like *this*. And I see the ice in you which puts a mountaintop to shame. And I think you should be very, very careful. Because there will come a moment, one crucial moment, where that makes it easy. That's all I need. One moment, to make the right decision where I made the wrong one all the other times. Go on, try me. Give me that moment. Put us both out of our bloody misery, if it means something but changes nothing. If it changes nothing, then you and I are headed for disaster, and I will *not* fail my friends again."

Nightingale's body fidgets under their hold. Her eyes are unblinking all the while, holding Lark's.

"Well," she breathes, barely audible. "That will be an interesting moment, indeed."

"Interesting?" Lark growls. They shake her, her body hitting the stone with a thud. "That's the best word you've got? Our friendship of years is headed for total destruction and you're calmly telling me it sounds *interesting*?!"

"Anything about you fascinates me, darling, it's just the way of things," Nightingale replies, unfazed by the violence. She sighs. "What do you want me to say? Do you want me to get angry? Shout at you?"

"I want you to *care*," Lark says, and they hate how their body is trembling. "Everything is falling apart. The world, and the war, and our home, and us—and I want you to care. There is so much to be angry about. And of all times, this is when you're *not* angry."

"Oh, I'm angry," Nightingale murmurs. She flips them so Lark is against the wall instead of her, so fast she catches them off guard. Lark's head rattles as it collides with the wall, and perhaps that is why their vision swims as Nightingale puts a leg between Lark's thighs to push herself further into their space, so that she can lean in close and whisper in their ear. "I walk alone in the world. I gave up everything to have a chance to find anything I wished, and that would have been fine but... I was imprisoned. By the one person left in the world I give a shit about. And now, although I'm out of my cell, I'm on a silly errand which has almost gotten me killed, because that's what my conspirators wanted in exchange for my freedom. So I'm not really free at all, yet, until I get them what they want. Consider me *furious*."

Lark has to struggle and twist their head to meet her eyes. They're so close they can taste her breath, hot and tinged with iron. "Who are they? Why protect them, if you don't want to be on their leash?"

"I'm on no one's leash," Nightingale snarls. "I'm fulfilling my end of a bargain, and then I'll either go on my way, or let them convince me to help with their bizarre little project."

"What project?" Lark swallows and forces out the next question. "Not the Ascension Project, is it?"

Nightingale's head tilts. Those lilac eyes are so guarded, so impossible to bypass to plunder the feelings locked away. She had certainly known something of the project, and of Palla the champion of the Warbringer's involvement, when they had been in Kequm. But as for anything else...

"Who could say?" she asks. Something sparks in her eyes. "Tell you what. I have a proposition. I was investigating ancient sites of power, when you arrested me. There's one not far from here, one I never got to. Some of the places, they're like the one we went to. They can make people *more*, open the magic to them... I think one of the people who helped me escape might be like us. There's something not right with the town near the ruin, and I don't know which one has the answers but I am sure that *one* of them does. If you go, and find a way to link what you find to a Disciplined mage in Kequm... then we can trade. You can confirm my theory, and I'll tell you who's up to no good there. The town's called Vincium."

Lark might usually struggle to win a physical contest with anyone. But this is Nightingale, and a greatly injured one at that. They wriggle free of her so that they can stare at her with the full force of every bit of incredulity in their body.

"What kind of trade is that?" Lark asks. "You give me the damning information I want, and all I have to do is prove some mage is like us? What does that matter?"

"Because they'll have better secrets to eat than anyone in that city," Nightingale says, as if it's obvious. "And if they're involved in a plot, I'd be practically helping you out by getting rid of them. Their magic is no joke, you want them out of your way."

"Oh really?"

The glint in her eyes strikes a new chord of worry in Lark's chest.

"Did you never wonder about the dragon, Lark?" Nightingale asks, with a girlish giggle. "The dragon that flew over right when I needed to escape again? Did that never strike you as incredibly convenient?"

Lark blinks. It's obvious now that she says it, and a thousand curses run through their mind as they resist the urge to clutch their hair and scream.

"The mage?" they ask.

"It wasn't real." Nightingale gives them an exhausted grin. "It was an illusion. That's why it didn't attack—it couldn't. It was all to buy me the two seconds I needed to escape that annoying champion."

"That kind of illusion—"

"Is huge and intricate and would have taken a disgusting amount of time and skill to prepare, yes," Nightingale says. "So now do you see? Why we need to learn more?"

"So what? Now we're on the same *side*? Do you even hear yourself?" Lark demands.

"I wouldn't go that far, darling. Hard to be on the same side when you're determined to arrest me." She adjusts her glasses, and then her jacket, smoothing wrinkles that Lark cannot even see. "But when I beat you today, and I will, I have no designs to be in your way. I'm on my own side. It doesn't have to be against yours. We can have common enemies, even."

"Unless you decide you like their side," Lark says, crossing their arms.

"Well, they *are* a fascinating bunch. Far more driven by purpose and innovation than most in Kequm. And... I'm sorry."

Lark blinks. Stares. Searches her eyes for deception only to find sympathy and sincerity where Lark had thought they were no longer permitted. "You're *what*?"

"I'm sorry, in advance," Nightingale says, more gently. "Because when I tell you who they are, it won't be easy for you to hear."

Maybe not officially, Wren had said about the possibility of the Bishops agreeing to enlist someone like Nightingale to help them with the Ascension Project. *You know. As a group. But maybe one of them did. Maybe they're planning on lying about where they got it. Things are getting desperate.*

"I can assure you, whatever you have to tell me can't be worse than things you've already said to me," Lark says, their fists clenched at their sides. They pause a moment and turn it over in their head, the proposition and the logic and which parts are the most essential. "I'll think about it. This is all assuming we don't capture you today, anyway."

"All good points," Nightingale agrees, like they're concluding an amicable business meeting.

"I think with every minute that passes, I understand you less," Lark says, not entirely meaning to voice it out loud. "I think that might be one of the saddest things in the world."

"If the only person who understands me no longer does, do I become an unfathomable unknown?" Nightingale smiles slightly. "How appropriate."

"No," Lark says. "You become lonely."

The smile slips. "Well. You would know."

The silence that follows is one of the worst in Lark's life. The tangle of vulnerability and resentment twists in the small space between them, the lingering care and connection that persists making it slick and dangerous and uncertain. It always comes back to the same question. *Where do we go from here?*

Today, at least, there is a geographical answer in place of a real one.

"Let's keep moving," Lark says with a sigh. The last thing they need is for Wren and Reverie, if they are indeed behind them, to catch up and walk right into this catastrophe of a conversation. Or, if it's finished rebuilding itself, the damned snake.

The energy of the walk is as strange as ever. They are truly cursed twice over, by the magic of the world itself and by each other, unable to let each other go and unable to truly meet in the middle.

A corner comes, and when they turn it, there is a wall with no gem. No, not a wall. A door.

"Oh," Lark says. "We're here."

"Oh," Nightingale whispers. "I see."

They approach together. The last brazier, this one above the door frame, lights at their proximity. The doors open of their own accord. Lark never knows what to expect from elven ruins, as the few they've had the pleasure to grace are always so different to one another.

Whatever they might have briefly imagined, however, is nothing close to the reality. A pedestal stands in the centre of the room, boasting an orb which glows bright green. Around it... is nothing short of a sanctuary. Life blooms here where it has no right to, roots coming through cracks in the stone and supporting trees and vines growing on a number of bizarre angles. It is one of the most beautiful places Lark has ever seen.

Nightingale is similarly agape. It is a rare thing to see her taken aback. But then the moment is gone, and her eyes move to Lark's. The orb glows in their periphery. It is the beacon signaling a change, a next step.

They have made it to the centre. And with that, their temporary alliance shatters.

Interlude

III - FERDINAND

FEW THINGS CREATED BY mortals bring joy to the cursed creature now known as Ferdinand. There's donuts, for their sheer perfection, raisin cookies for the misery they bring mortals who mistake them for something else, and the sound of a wind instrument in the hands of an incompetent.

The gong of failure is becoming a strong contender. Each failure—and there have been several—has been a delight, but the latest has brought out something new.

A full body freeze. Tears so silent they are somehow gloriously worse. All of it brought on by her own weakness? Glorious.

He's only been back on the mortal plane for around twenty minutes. It's absolutely worth it to have the chance to cackle at the two despondent women he's stuck following around, and he knows he will be chastised and no doubt banished once again. He held it together first, for the sake of his petty plan, but now as the last seconds of the minute waiting period close in, he can let out his mirth to echo.

What better, than to waste a little more of their time? It takes only a powerful singular flap to launch himself into the air towards the trial gem so that he can fail it and force out another waiting period.

Contact. The trial speaks to him, and for someone with a permanent telepathic link with another, it should be less jarring but is not. *Our tethers to those that walk this world with us are what give us perspective and balance. You may pass if you possess a bond with someone strong enough that it will only be broken by death.*

Ferdinand squawks in mocking, his mouth locked around the damned gem. As if he could ever have a bond with one of these pathetic mortals, as if he wouldn't have ground them to pieces and used their bones for toothpicks—

The gem pulses, and the wall vanishes.

Ferdinand stares. Stares, and wonders if after all these centuries, he is finally losing his tiny goose mind now that his superior one has been crammed into it for so long.

A bond broken only by death.

He looks to Reverie, the person he is fated to follow until she expires.

Well, sure, *technically*.

He is dispatched once again with an irritated snap of Reverie's fingers, and is sure to call her a bitch one more time as he is yanked back to his tedious pocket plane.

Chapter 10

For once in their life, Lark has the guts to attack first. They shout a brief cry to the Scholar and throw their hand up into Nightingale's face. From it flares light so bright she can only stumble back from it, blinded. Lark shoves her into the doorframe and grabs her wrists, pulling rope from their pocket and beginning to tie her up.

An elbow rams Lark's chin. Then, a shoe heel kicks their knee so hard that Lark's leg gives out and falls on their side. Before they can recover, cold darkness covers their mouth and nose, blocking airflow.

No, Lark thinks. *Not again.* They had been so close, finally. So close to getting it right.

The rope finds their wrists. Lark tries to fight, kicking and wriggling, but with every moment passing their attempts grow weaker as their head spins from lack of oxygen. Nightingale presses her knee into their back, tying them awkwardly, perhaps with one hand.

"You look good like this," she says when she's finished. The darkness drops from Lark's face and they are too busy gasping for breath to give her a flustered reaction to such a comment. The binder makes oxygen hard to find.

Nightingale smirks regardless, satisfied in her victory one way or another, and she turns to head for the orb.

"Gorgeous," she whispers to the orb. "Alright. Better get going."

With a glance towards the open door, Nightingale grabs the artifact in the crook of her arm and teleports up to one of the tree branches high above, ten feet above the ground. She straddles it and reaches into one of her larger pockets in the bottom of her long jacket, pulling out her stolen Wayfinder. It's identical to Lark's, in all but a small numeral which will be etched into the top. Lark's reads *eleven*.

Orb still secured in her elbow nook, Nightingale holds the Wayfinder with both hands. Lark can see her mouth moving but cannot make out the words she utters to activate it. Gold, shimmering magic covers the device and Lark curses everything, wishing they had a way to stop her, a way to do anything that isn't just lie here and watch and fail *again*—

Soft hands touch Lark's wrists. Their head shoots around and meets golden eyes, while their binds tug and fall away. Reverie smiles, holding up her ornate dagger to twirl once in her fingers. Lark has never been so relieved to see her often infuriating face. They sit up and rub their wrists, seeking Wren and finding her running for the tree Nightingale has holed up in.

Classic Wren. But if Lark has their timing right, there's no way she'll reach it before—

A flash of gold. Then, a bewildered curse.

Nightingale, still very much present, stares at her empty hands. No orb. No Wayfinder. "What the *fuck*?!"

"Oh," Lark says, as if that syllable will encapsulate bafflement and screaming curiosity in any measure.

"Did they—" Nightingale shakes herself. "No, I grabbed my own, they never—" Her eyes snap to Lark. Sharp. Deadly. Different, now that she's desperate and on the back foot. "Nevermind."

Oh *no*. There is one other way for her to make a quick getaway, and it's weighing heavy on Lark's back.

Wren, about to start climbing the tree, looks at Lark as Nightingale vanishes into a portal and reappears just in time to get her hand smacked away by Lark when she goes for their backpack.

"Nope," they say. "That's not yours, dear—"

Another portal. Another whirl around. Like a twisted game of stone, parchment and shears, only with left, right and same place. Nightingale makes fevered grabs for the backpack and Lark manages to keep shaking her off. Reverie hovers nearby, dagger still in hand and eyes darting fast, but her body frozen.

Nightingale teleports right in front of Lark. A fascinating strategy, one they try to unravel in the split second they have to react, because how is she going to—

Karma can be a bitch. This is about all Lark can think, as Nightingale tackles them to the ground and their hips painfully collide with stone. A roll, then a pull at their back, and Lark shouts but they just can't see her. But even if she gets the Wayfinder, she doesn't have the—

"No," Lark says, the danger dawning on them in the moment she teleports next to Reverie. "Nightingale, please—"

Nightingale's eyes have no warmth left for them. Her gaze is like steel. She might not have the password... but she can extract it from any one of them.

A portal opens behind her, and Nightingale wraps her arm around Reverie's shoulders, yanking her towards it. Lark and Wren shout in protest, but neither can reach them in the split second where it matters.

"Oh, fuck off!" Reverie tells Nightingale. Her boots dig into the floor right as Nightingale pulls at her, and she barely moves an inch. The portal snaps shut right after, unused.

Reverie snaps her fingers. A furious, honking goose appears right in front of Nightingale's face, forcing out a shout of alarm. Something shifts in Reverie's eyes. She turns with astounding speed and does *something*, but Lark can't see a damned thing but goose wings and feathers.

Nightingale staggers back from Reverie, eyes wide and panicked, her free hand coming to a new, bleeding wound in her side. Wren runs for her, sword ready, but Nightingale teleports back into the tree on her own. Reverie makes an odd noise and touches a bloody tear in her shirt.

"I think I got her better," Reverie says, staring at the blood on the fingers of her free hand. "Huh."

Lark hurries to her side and gets to healing it before they can find out how bad the wound is. Meanwhile, Wren stalks the same few feet while staring up at Nightingale, like a panther debating how to reach a bird in the canopy.

"Now what?" Wren asks, craning her neck up and huffing with inordinate frustration.

So much has happened today. Lark and Nightingale have staggered their way through the labyrinth, but the wear of the snake's attacks and the force of the self-destruct explosion have taken its toll on them both. Nightingale is only functional because of Lark's magic, and they do feel a specific sort of awful about that, but this new wound is serious business.

Nightingale shoves Lark's Wayfinder into her pocket and rummages in another for a small potion she gulps down.

"This is our chance to get her," Wren says. "I can climb the tree, but she's got teleport magic."

"She must be running low," Lark tells her. "But one wrong move, and she kills one of you for the Wayfinder's passphrase. We can't let that happen."

Wren groans. "I can't do nothing!"

"Not nothing, just... not the wrong thing," Lark says, but it does little to satisfy her. They glance at Reverie, who is busy staring at the bloody dagger in her hand and doesn't appear to be listening. Then, her head snaps towards the goose at her feet. She scowls and wipes the blood onto his feathers. There is a great honking protest but he doesn't actually move, making Lark think he has been commanded to comply.

Reverie finally looks up at Lark. "That was nearly—"

Noise down the corridor distracts Lark from her words. It's difficult to place and immediately sets Lark's body on edge with its dissonance and ever growing volume. They run for the door and look out of it.

A metal shape is slithering across the stone, coming in fast.

"Ah," Lark says, dashing back into the centre of the room. "That lack of humility is about to be a problem, dear," they call to Nightingale. She glares and continues her makeshift first aid on herself.

"Wait, why?" Wren asks.

"Well, the snake targeted her last time," Lark explains. "And she's failed more trials since, so she's the obvious target."

The colour drains from Wren's face.

"What if someone else failed? More recently?" she asks.

Before Lark can answer, the snake bursts into the room and tries to devour Wren in one gulp.

Chapter 11

Lark has learned a few things about how Wren reacts in a crisis since making her acquaintance. One: Wren has an admirable ability to keep a cool head when things go wrong. Two: Wren knows her strengths and will utilise them in an excellent manner. Three: Wren knows something that many who are supposedly more clever—such as Lark themself—struggle to get correct. Wren knows when to run.

She bolts for the exit passage after rolling out of the way of the snake's bite, and draws her sword as she runs, ready to use it to fend off the teeth and gaping mouth.

Lark can think of nothing better to do than to grab Reverie and follow Wren's exemplary lead.

"Give me the passphrase, Lark!" Nightingale calls from her perch. "Or do you want me to die in here?"

It might be the longest moment of Lark's life, then. Staring up at her, wondering if they can really condemn her *or* save her, if they could justify either. A week ago, Lark might have spent an hour agonising over it, but they do not have an hour. Wren might have seconds, and Lark has one of the only definitive ways to get away from the damned snake.

Help Nightingale? Or leave her to die?

Or... neither.

"The snake isn't after you," Lark says, and the clarity comes like soothing water over agitated wounds. "And you still have magic left. You wanted me to go to Vincium, to the ruin, so I'll take the south road. You take the north. Wouldn't recommend following us as both of my friends have pointy objects with your name on them."

Nightingale scowls, and Lark tips an imaginary hat in her direction.

"See you in Kequm, dear."

They run out before she can respond, before her face can shift from inscrutable stillness into something that may dissuade them from the closest thing to sense they've felt in years. The snake is taking up a decent portion of the exit tunnel, but with it facing Wren and Wren doing an absolutely marvellous job of fighting off the damned thing, it is easy enough to slip past.

Wren's face is fierce and determined as she parries every attack with her greatsword, her stance strong and unwavering. Unlike Lark and Nightingale, her body is unfatigued from the day and braced for a challenge.

"We need to run," Lark says to Reverie, because Wren's eyes are occupied. "All of us!"

"That's gonna be tricky," Wren says, locking her sword against a row of teeth and groaning as she forces the construct to recoil.

I know, Lark tries to say while looking at Reverie, but the words don't come out, as Reverie is not the intended recipient. Absurd clever magic.

They pull out their last two boom balls. "Better get this right," they say to Reverie, and the smile that has sprung to their face might be manic with adrenaline. "Tell her to duck."

"Wren, duck... *now*!" Reverie shouts, right as Lark throws the first boom ball in a calculated arc over Wren's head and into the snake's open mouth.

"Lark, was that one of your fucking—"

"Run!" Lark shouts as soon as her incredulous eyes whip around to meet theirs.

Wren barely has time to scramble away as the boom ball explodes. The snake jerks at a jarring angle, giving them a few more precious seconds to get distance from it, running as fast as their legs can carry them.

One more shot, before it recovers. Lark murmurs a prayer, not for magic but simply for luck and guidance, and throws the second one at the ceiling above the snake's head. Contact. Rupture. The ceiling of the tunnel caves in over the snake's head, burying it.

The trio continue to run.

"Will that hold it?" Wren asks.

"Don't know," Lark tells her, with an exhaled laugh. "Hopefully it's tied to the labyrinth, which means we just need to get out."

Lark makes it another three minutes until exhaustion and their binder team up to bring them to their knees. They pant helplessly, hands planted against the rough cobbles.

"What happened to you, anyway?" Wren asks, as she lifts them to their feet. "You look like shit."

"Oh! I got blown up," Lark says brightly.

"*What?*"

"Turns out the snake has a self-destruct mechanism designed to take out anyone who manages to defeat it," Lark continues, taking Wren's horrified question as permission. "So when I threw a boom ball into its power core, it exploded so badly it knocked me out through my shield."

"But it's back there! Don't tell me there's *another* one—"

"Of course not, it seems to have a self-repair function. But yes." Lark coughs into their hand as Wren's expression becomes even less amused. "That's why Nightingale's looking awful too, even pre-stabbing."

"Sorry," Reverie interjects. "Or, I mean, I'm not—" She makes a face. "I don't know if I am. I've never stabbed anyone before. Not for real. But she was... going to kill me."

"Yes, she was," Lark replies as they meet her gaze evenly. Now is not the time to mince words. "You did what you felt was right. You'll see no criticism from me, Rosetia."

Reverie nods, even more so when Wren pats her on the shoulder.

"I think I should just carry you," Wren says to Lark. "You'll slow us down, otherwise."

Lark glances at Wren's shoulders, then at her face which is devoid of judgement and holds only pragmatism. Well, the day hadn't been huge on dignity regardless. This won't be much of a step down.

"Yes, alright. Probably for the best."

Which is how Lark rides out of the Labyrinth on Wren's shoulders, watching a quieter-than-usual Reverie put her dagger into her thigh sheath and waiting to see if she'll start an argument for fun. No such thing occurs.

They're all a bit shaken, Lark supposes. Once they're back to their debates, that will be how they'll know everything is well again.

Daylight is a relief to the eyes and heart, after so much time in the sallow green light of the Labyrinth's passages. The dark is an eerie thing when tainted by green, whereas when the colour graces the day, the source is rolling hills and grasses that cover them. Lark could kiss them.

"Oh! We're right by the entrance," they say when they come out near a familiar part of the hill, and can see Melora's pale gold flank shining in the sun. "There we go. Let's keep moving."

Reverie is quick to fetch her loyal steed, and they make their way from the Labyrinth as quickly as possible while keeping a sustainable pace. All they need to do is get far enough away that the deconstructed snake and an injured Nightingale are no longer immediate dangers. Reverie rides Melora while Wren continues to carry Lark for the sake of speed.

After five minutes in the fresh air, with no rumbling behind them signalling trouble in the form of a serpent construct, it is even easier to breathe.

They've lived to stumble through another day.

"We might be able to get another horse and a double saddle from the next town," Lark muses to Reverie. "Wherever that is."

"You'll have to ride with me," Reverie says. "Wren's armour will be too heavy for a double up."

"Yes, yes, no need to sound so excited," Lark snorts.

Wren makes a face. "If I'm going to be on a horse, it'll need to be a nice one. I'm not a great rider."

"Oh, horses are easy!" Lark tells her. You just have to treat them like large and intuitive people, with much scarier back legs."

"Right," Wren says, still looking dubious, but with a thoughtful spark in her eye.

It's a tip which helped Lark immensely, back when the general size of horses and their tendency to overthink anything had made for a near-lethal combination any time they attempted mounting. Now, Lark will happily chat to any horse as if they're another person along for the journey, but can only do so when looking in their eyes. Curious, how their curse applies to animals as well as people. But then, what difference is there between a horse and a person in the eyes of cosmic energy? A small difference in limbs, but semi-similar arrangement and dietary needs.

All the same, Lark would pay almost any price in the world to be able to read a guidebook on the rules of said cosmic energy. Possibly even one of their hands, which are not essential for cosmic energy guidebook reading.

"We're going east, right?" Reverie asks Lark, who realises that she certainly heard them mention Vincium and absolutely knows where it is.

"Are we? Back to Kequm?" Wren asks.

"That general direction, yes," Lark says, without elaborating further, in the hopes of resting a little longer before a difficult conversation.

Reverie, for whatever reason, keeps quiet about whatever she overheard.

The three of them continue on their new path for several hours, chewing on travel rations as they go, until a shimmering image appears in thin air right ahead of them.

Chapter 12

THE IMAGE IS A person. Or rather, two people.

Andrian, the deputy Bishop of the Scholar, and Lark's old schoolmate. With him is Cillian, the emergency admin of Kequm. In person they would make for a picture of contrasts: Andrian's short stature and closely cropped dark hair next to Cillian's tall and slender form and flowing blonde hair which reaches all the way to his waist. Here (or rather, not here at all) there are no colours, only different shimmering shades of a silvery hue. Cillian's hand rests on Andrian's shoulder, connecting them to the Deputy to enable their connection to the spell.

Some Gifted mages can master long-distance communication between themself and another person. It is usually only a verbal connection, and even *that* is considered a moderately difficult feat. Developing it to the point of creating a visual to go with it is uncommon and greatly respected.

But then, Andrian is a Gifted mage of great power, between clairvoyance and this. They all have their strengths; while Lark has never managed to pull off even verbal communication over distance and certainly not for lack of trying, Andrian has never been able to heal anyone let alone regrow missing flesh.

Lark has seen this show of Andrian's abilities before. They had been chasing Nightingale then, too.

"Lark!" Andrian says. "I've been trying to reach you all day. I had the most awful vision of you—"

"Really? That's strange, you should have been able to reach me," Lark says, glancing back towards the Labyrinth with puzzlement. Their magic worked fine in the Labyrinth, and so had Nightingale's. Andrian, being of the same Gifted nature, shouldn't have had any trouble unless something is built into the Labyrinth's exterior which prevents magic from penetrating from the outside. But what would be the point of that?

"Lark, who are you talking to?" Wren asks.

"Oh, Andrian, he's got this marvellous projection spell thing," Lark says. "If you could put me down? You two can rest while we talk."

Wren obliges and Lark is able to get themself vertical again with a modicum of dignity. Cillian looks amused, which Lark chooses to ignore. Reverie and Wren exchange bemused looks at Lark's words, but do not discard the chance to rest.

Because the spell touches Lark's mind directly, through their connection to Andrian, no one can see the projection but Lark. Magic is an odd, specific thing.

Lark considers Andrian curiously. "I wonder why you couldn't—"

"I've reached you now, that's what matters," Andrian says. Wise of him, not to let Lark get into another ramble about magic's unpredictable nature. "How goes the search for Nightingale?"

Lark blinks at him. "You... told me not to go after Nightingale, Andrian. You threatened to strip me of my title if I interfered with anyone trying to capture her."

"Well, *have* you interfered with anyone else trying to capture her?" Andrian asks, with a lift of his eyebrow.

"Well, no—"

"Because no one has been dispatched. It's been a bit of a hard sell, and we have other needs of the few mercenaries around," Andrian says with a sigh. "Besides. I never expected you to stay away. But my position demands certain expectations be set."

"I understand," Lark says, and it is mostly true. They glance at Cillian. "Is there a particular reason you're here, Cillian? I can see why you'd be working closely with Andrian on a number of things, but this matter is perhaps—"

"Please forgive the intrusion, Seeker," Cillian says, voice soft as he glances at Andrian, who has gone stiff. "The deputy here is under far more stress than he would have you know. By happy, if unexpected, coincidence, he finds my presence to be a comfort."

His hand strokes over the fabric of Andrian's robe where it rests on his shoulder, and even through the silvery wash Lark can see Andrian's cheeks darkening as his eyes fix firm on his feet.

"Oh, I see," Lark says. "Andrian, that's nothing to be embarrassed about, for the Scholar's sake. You're fighting a war. You're allowed to need support."

"Lark, we've never once discussed my personal life, I'd prefer not to start now," Andrian says through his teeth.

"Excellent then we shan't. What was that vision about me, then?"

"The vision involved you finding Nightingale, today," Andrian says. "Is that what happened? Where is she?"

Lark sighs. The shame is back, that sense of failure thrumming through their veins. "She was after some sort of artifact, a magical amplifier hidden in a ruin here in central Qelandia. But when she tried to leave with her Wayfinder, it only took the amplifier. Not her. So she took *my* Wayfinder. We barely escaped before she could get the password out of us, but Wren and our new friend here managed to do enough of a number on her that I don't think she'll be following us."

"So you have no Wayfinder, and she has one she can't use?" Andrian asks, with visible shock.

"I know, I know, I'm sorry—"

"Lark, at least you're safe," Andrian says. His relief washes over Lark with surprising warmth, like an older brother they'd never had. "Did you get a sense of where she was planning to go?"

"Back to Kequm, to whoever helped her escape, was the impression I got. With the Wayfinder mishap... I don't know."

"Will you follow her?"

Lark thinks of Nightingale's bizarre proposition and their even more strange half-promise to see it through, if only to keep them on different paths so that Wren and Reverie keep breathing. It is impossible to remember that conversation without also recalling her preemptive apology about revealing who has been helping her.

If Wren is in any way right about one of the Bishops being responsible for this mess, the only person who might be even more reluctant to hear it than Lark... would be Andrian. There is no way to explain Nightingale's strange offer of near partnership without sounding like a traitor.

"I think it's in everyone's best interests that I keep myself and my friends away from her, so she's forced to return to Kequm on foot. We'll do the same, and try to deal with her once we're back."

"Good, good," Andrian says. "We do need your help here, Lark. Rather desperately. But you won't be able to provide that help if you don't arrive safely. Ensure that's your top priority."

"Need my help with what?"

"Something's wrong here, but it's hard to determine what or why," Cillian answers. "It could be the war getting the best of people, wartime morale, but... it feels like more than that. Workers on the Ascension Project are having nightmares and even—"

"Cillian," Andrian interrupts. "We can explain once they arrive."

"Yes, of course." Cillian straightens their back and coughs into their free hand. "Just... hurry back, Seeker."

"If you're in central Qelandia, it'll be quite a trek." Andrian looks pensive. "I'll check in once a week. Check you're alright, and on track."

"Sounds good," Lark says. "Stay safe, Andrian. And you, Cillian. Thank you for—" Lark makes a face and gestures vaguely in Andrian's direction. "He's never been good at letting other people help him. I appreciate it."

Cillian grins. "Well, I'm nothing if not persistent."

Lark can only laugh at that. "Talk in a week, then. Both of you."

"Indeed," Andrian says, back to looking mortified, and the two of them flicker out of sight as the spell's connection severs.

Reverie and Wren are sitting in the dirt, faces open and expectant by the time Lark turns around.

"That was really weird," Wren says. "And you think I'd stop saying that, or get used to there always being something strange, but I keep... not."

"Yes, very uncommon magic, that little trick," Lark says with a grin. "Can you imagine? And we have to send letters if we want to talk to people across hundreds of miles."

"So who's Andrian, anyway?" Reverie asks.

"Deputy Bishop of the Temple of the Scholar," Wren answers, before Lark can. "Apparently he and Lark went to school together."

Reverie lifts an eyebrow. "So like... your boss?"

"We're not a *guild*, it's more nuanced than that and—" Lark deflates. "And you were joking." Reverie nods, a shit-eating grin on her lips, and Lark pinches the bridge of their nose. "Right. Anyway. He was checking in, because on top of top-tier communication magic, the thing he's actually known for is his clairvoyance. He'd had a vision about me, so he wanted to check in."

"If he gets visions of the future, you think he'd get a vision warning him Nightingale was going to escape in the first place," Wren says.

Lark shakes their head. "It's not an *alert* service. You have to ask specific questions, and—"

"I'd just ask if there was going to be any danger in the city that day," Reverie says with a shrug. "Surely that would cover those kinds of bases. You could build a news team around it. No nasty surprises."

"Gifted magic needs a specific target, such as himself or me," Lark reminds her. "You can't just inquire about a whole city. Too broad."

"True," Reverie says. She looks disappointed and starts pulling at the grass near her knees and tearing it apart between her fingers. "So what was the vision?"

"Well—" Lark stops. "We got a bit sidetracked from that. He was more worried about us, than anything. And about where Nightingale is. You can't blame him."

"I got the sense we're now allowed to be chasing her, again," Wren says slowly. "Is that a good idea?"

"We're not going to chase her, but there is... you know. The matter of transport."

"You said we're going back to Kequm, by the south road," Reverie says. "You said to Nightingale that we'd go to Vincium, to a ruin. Because she wanted to. What the fuck was *that* about?"

"You said *what*?!" Wren demands.

"Wren, before you quite rightly hold me accountable to my questionable decisions, please do hear me out, and you can make your own call," Lark is quick to say.

Being the remarkable person she is, Wren closes her mouth and waits. On any other day, Lark might be taken by the picture she creates, leaning back on her hands in the shine of the sun, the breeze moving through her short curls and flower blossoms. Patience and strength, radiant in the sun.

Lark swallows. More than anything, they will try to avoid Wren's disappointment.

"She offered a bit of a compromise—ridiculous, I know, but let me continue—and unfortunately everything she said made perfect sense. She claims to not be the mastermind behind her escape, that the artifact was to be payment for her freedom. She suspects a number of things at work. At the forefront, a mage with the capability to weave illusions of an astronomical complexity."

At that, Reverie's eyebrows shoot up. "Like the ones in the Collection?"

Lark goes to answer in the negative, only to stop. "Well, actually, her example was the dragon that flew over us in Kequm. Apparently it was an illusion. But now that you mention it... we said perhaps the reason we ended up in the Collection was an unseen connection. This person may be the very thing. The magic there said it was an echo of someone real, someone who looked to change the world..."

It's a curious thing, to feel as though two puzzle pieces have clicked together, only for the full picture to remain as unclear as before.

"If it's a mage, it would explain why they want a magical amplifier," Wren points out.

"Exactly," Lark agrees. "Nightingale wants to... trade. Information. She claims not to be part of the conspiracy, yet. She's wary of this mage's power, and thinks they're like... well. Us. Myself and her. Able to see things others can't. Given powers beyond the usual. She says if we can confirm this, she'll lead us to her conspirators *and* take the mage out of the equation. Which *might* be something we want, depending on what these people are actually planning on doing."

"Why does she think we're going to find that proof there?" Reverie asks.

"... she wouldn't tell me that part," Lark says, making a face. "Classic Nightingale. She has to see if we can figure out whatever *she* did. All she would say is that the ruin is like the one that changed *us*, and that there's something wrong with the town near it. But Vincium *is* on the way to Kequm anyway. So... what do we think?"

"I say we go," Reverie says. "There are way too many questions and no answers."

Wren is silent. Her eyes move between Lark and Reverie and the horizon behind the former.

"I figured if I said we might go, and told her to take the other road, she was more likely to leave us alone if she thinks we're running her errand," Lark adds, nervously. Their hands are twisted in front of them, resting on the bottom of their waistcoat.

"This feels like a wild puzzle chase designed to keep you out of her business," Wren says eventually. "It took literally one minute to catch Reverie in the same trap."

Reverie opens her mouth to argue only to shut it again, shrug, and go back to shredding grass.

"But," Wren continues, "As much as I fucking hate to say it... too much of it is making sense. I'd been wondering about the dragon, I realised how it didn't attack when I was talking to Norak. If it was an illusion, it couldn't. Right?"

"Brilliant," Lark says. "You're *brilliant*. I never gave it a second thought."

"You were having a bad day," Wren points out. "And I forgot almost right after I realised, because *I* was having a bad day. And I still hate this."

"Good! I think we're all much safer if you do." Lark grins when their words pull a chuckle from Wren's throat. "Is that a yes?"

"So, prove a murderous bitch right by solving another mystery, to barter for information on wartime conspiracy," Wren says to Reverie. "That's what you want to do?"

"That's one of the sexiest sentences I've ever heard," Reverie exhales with great melodrama. "Obviously."

"If I see her again, she's getting friendly with my sword," Wren promises Lark. "No one is getting stabbed again on my watch."

Lark pulls them both to their feet and embraces them tightly, one in each arm. Wren hugs back with one strong arm, while Reverie stiffens at first but pats Lark on the back several times before they pull away. After everything that happened inside the

Labyrinth, the safety of an embrace with friends does wonders for Lark's battered heart.

"We can do this," Lark says, before striding off down the path. They hope the more they say it, the more they'll believe it. Things with Nightingale are far from finished, but today Lark took a step towards choosing the right thing over choosing Nightingale. It's a start.

And so they press on. Leaving one ancient ruin to seek out another, treading through places of the past in the hopes it will shed light on the uncertain and shadowy future.

Lark has never felt more like the Seeker they swore to be, and never been so terrified about what truths might be found.

TO BE CONTINUED IN

VOLUME V: THE SPIRIT TORMENTS

Afterword

And with that, that's Act 1 of 3 of Catastrophe Incoming at a close. Act 2 will open with Volume V bringing in a new character, our final POV, Lanan! I can't wait for you all to meet him. *The Spirit Torments* will be out in October 2024.

If you enjoyed this book and the ones before it, I would be really grateful if you would consider leaving me a review on Goodreads and Amazon, as it really helps me out as an indie author.

If you'd like to read more from me, you can get a FREE BOOK, a fantasy mystery novelette called *The Curious Matter of Myron Manor,* if you sign up to my newsletter! Head to www.aimeedonnellan.com/newsletter or you can scan the QR code over the page.

If you'd like to find me on social media, you can find me on Twitter / X as @bardqueenaimee.

Everywhere else I am @aimeedonnellanwrites!

Acknowledgements

I am so excited to say we've done it again! This series is blooming, and I couldn't have done it without the incredible little team that has stuck alongside me. My betas Bryanna, Senka and Norah, my editor Quinn, and the members of my Aboria Archivists discord who are always there to cheer me on and help me out with little things. I couldn't do this without you. To my writing pals Caitlin, Keanna and Pragnya: thank you for being your wonderful, hilarious, supportive selves all the time. I love being your friend.

To Ty: the journey to this book has been some of the most challenging in the aspects of our everyday life, as we battle everything our minds and bodies throw at us from injuries to random slumps to accidentally getting back into Darkest Dungeon II. I love you, I couldn't do this without your help all week every week, and I love the world you made for us to play around with. Thank you for everything, always.

To my coworkers: it's not likely you'll read this, but thank you for making my day job a delight. This wouldn't be possible if I didn't have a day job that keeps me busy and social and filled with inspiration. You're the best team I could ask to be a part of.

Kate, thank you for the amazing art as always. I cannot WAIT to for us to get into Lanan's design for the next cover.

To Jas from Wellington, I don't know if you tend to read this far, but I hope you do. Your family coming to see me at Wellington Pride and telling me how much you loved my books might be the most special moment for me in my author journey so far. I wrote this series exactly for people like you, and me, and I hope with everything that I have that you continue to love it.

And to anyone else who has read this far, thanks for coming along for the ride, and I hope you join Lark and Reverie and Wren on the rest of their adventure.

The adventure continues in
VOLUME V: THE SPIRIT TORMENTS

Turn the page for a special preview!

Lanan knows the situation is getting serious when he's run out of ghost jokes. Or rather, that his levity has moved from a refreshing change of pace to a discordant presence.

The bottom floor of the Proud Steed, the only inn in the town of Vincium, is empty but for Lanan and the barkeep. After delivering Lanan his coffee and toast slathered in jam, the middle-aged human woman checks her counter stock with an occasional tired murmur to herself before a scribble in her logbook.

Lanan's good morning to her had been met with a disbelieving hum. Not the most inspiring of breakfast conversation.

It wouldn't be so disheartening, were it the only time they'd had this exchange. But today makes the third morning in a row she's said less than a single word.

Lanan sips his coffee while his left hand scribbles this information in his notebook. His cat, Remmie, watches with groggy half-interest where she is perched on the edge of the table.

"We'll *make* it a good morning, won't we, Remmie?" he says softly, in Elvish.

He gets a noncommittal meow in response. Quite fair.

Once he puts down his pen, his hand drifts down to the folded paper sitting in the left pocket of his loose trousers. He doesn't pull it out; he knows every word of the letter by heart.

It just seems important not to lose his reminder that in being here, he is delayed being elsewhere.

But the town of Vincium needs help, and no one else is here.

"Good morning, Vincium," he says when he strides out of the inn ten minutes later, leaving Remmie to her own devices.

He speaks to an empty town square, as per usual, but this seldom phases him. One cannot be phased when there is a central fountain with a ledge wide enough to be perfect for leaping onto. Humming to himself, he slides along the marble surface before spinning on the ball of his foot through his fitted leather boot.

His dance practice is falling a little to the wayside. It's not the most urgent of concerns, as choosing to trek across half the known world to check on a friend means he won't be initiated into the Chorus Guard for another couple of years. Still, he'll have to ensure he gets back to his morning practices once he's out of here.

Four more spins and a leap to the ground later, and Lanan is ready to begin making his rounds. Not for the first time since arriving in Vincium, he wishes he had taken the time to learn a musical instrument. There had been so much music, back in Shilheim, it had never occurred to him he would end up somewhere without it. He'd been so busy dancing, taking it all for granted.

He'd give anything to hear a new song, about now. But it's not about him. It's about the people of Vincium, until he works out how to set their hearts at ease.

"Good morning," he says to the baker, who is laying out the first of his loaves along his shop sill. "They all look marvellous."

The baker nods. There is no smile. He's a thick-set fellow with dark red hair, a few streaks of grey beginning to peek through at the hairline. There are lines at the corners of his mouth, as if from years of laughter.

Lanan wishes more than anything to see that laughter now. But he simply hands over a coin, takes a fresh roll, and continues down the street.

The elemental-blood children, their fiery hair visible and distinct from halfway down the street, run out of their house and begin passing a ball between them. Much slower, their mother comes to sit on the house step, keeping a tired but close eye.

As Lanan continues on, there are squeals as they spot him. "Lanan!"

They run to him, eyes ember bright. He ruffles the hair of the sister, a seven year old named Haley, and withdraws his hand before the heat from her glowing curls can burn him.

"Will you play with us?" her brother Arlo asks. He's four, a darling who never stops moving and always accidentally shouts.

Lanan accepts because it is impossible to deny such charming smiles. They throw the ball to each other while standing in a triangle formation, and Lanan intermittently checks on the children's mother when he has a spare few seconds.

The dark circles under her eyes have not impressed. She offers Lanan a miniscule smile of gratitude for his entertaining Haley and Arlo, but exhaustion keeps it from fully reaching her eyes.

"Are you two looking after your mother?" Lanan asks Haley.

"We are, we help with lots of things," Haley assures him. "But Ma keeps saying that stuff."

"Ma never used to be so mean," Arlo adds. "Just because you're dead, it's not okay to be mean."

Their other mother has been dead for a year. And, like any others who have passed, where her spirit ought to have moved on, it is lingering.

Lanan sighs. "I agree. I wish we knew what everyone's problem was. Then we could fix it and everyone could get some sleep."

"*I* still sleep," Arlo says, not sounding thrilled about it.

"Bedtime is important," his sister says. "If *you* get tired, you cry."

"I do not!"

Lanan throws the ball towards Arlo before it can turn into an argument. Arlo fumbles it and watches it bounce down the street for a moment before hurrying to fetch it.

"Should I walk you to school again?" Lanan asks them.

"Yes!"

Lanan looks to Grace to check for permission from her as well, and receives the same grateful approval through another nod and how she rises to re-enter her house.

The walk to the schoolhouse almost feels familiar now, and Lanan has only made it with Haley and Arlo three times including today. But he's sometimes come this way to check on the head schoolteacher, and only really needs to walk to a place once before it is locked in his memory forever.

"Bye Lanan!" Haley says as she tugs Arlo inside the quaint wooden building. Arlo waves goodbye and Lanan continues on his way.

There's a delightful tree just on the edge of the schoolyard, perfect for sitting under with a book. Just as Lanan gets himself settled with his textbook and notebook, ready for a small study session, Remmie meows to announce her presence as she strides up and settles herself against his side.

"Good walk?" he asks. Another meow. "I wonder if there's a spell I can learn to make you talk. That would be fun."

If a cat could look sceptical, Remmie would be just about there.

"Not that I'm not grateful for being able to make my hair look marvellous at any moment, or haven't found the gale force strikes useful in a pinch, but air is proving to be one of the *least* helpful elements for solving problems. At least fire creates warmth. Water creates puddles, which lead to splashing, and happy children. Best I can do is knock things over. No one here needs *that*."

Remmie licks his hand and he is quick to scritch behind her ears.

"I do sound ungrateful, don't I?" He sighs. "Sorry. But you're the prime example of what *one* instance of Disciplined magic can do. If only it didn't take so long to learn *one* spell."

He curls his right hand, where his focus rings decorate each finger, letting him channel the essence of air within him and push it out into a soft gust that hits the tree branches.

A leaf falls, wafting down to land on the tip of Lanan's finger. It would be a perfect moment of serenity if it were not broken by the most unexpected, bewildering noise to pierce a sedate Vincium morning.

The honk of a goose.

www.ingramcontent.com/pod-product-compliance
Lightning Source LLC
Chambersburg PA
CBHW021717190726
48289CB00008B/2568